"Did you really want to be free of me, Miss Devenish?"

"Oh, no, my lord!" Harriet's cry came from her heart. "I—I thought that it was you who wanted to be free of me!"

"What do you mean, Miss Devenish?"

"You said to Her Grace that I—I was an encumbrance!"

"But I did not mean—I had no wish to see you gone!"

"Oh!" Harriet felt like weeping, so happy did she suddenly feel.

"And you would permit me, Miss Devenish, to keep you safe always?" Lord Richard asked now, very tenderly.

"I have always felt safe with you, my lord."

The next moment, Harriet was in Lord Richard's embrace. . . .

FANCY FREE

Charlotte Grey

FAWCETT CREST • NEW YORK

A Fawcett Crest Book
Published by Ballantine Books
Copyright © 1984 by Charlotte Grey

First published in Great Britain 1984

Library of Congress Catalog Card Number: 87-91534

ISBN 0-449-21292-0

This edition published by arrangement with Robert Hale, Ltd.

Manufactured in the United States of America

First Ballantine Books Edition: October 1987

One

For as long as she could remember, Harriet Devenish had been a boarder at Miss Bassenthwaite's Academy for Young Ladies a short distance outside Carlisle. Throughout that time, money drafts from the London establishment of Drummonds had arrived with the expected banker's punctuality to pay for her board and lodging, clothes and education.

And the drafts had not been niggardly. Everything had been done in the most lavish manner: every extra of drawing and music, dancing and languages had been provided for the young lady, and the clothes Miss Bassenthwaite had been bidden to provide for her were to be of as good quality as were to be found in the whole of Cumberland, or indeed, the Border.

The only thing lacking was any sign of human agency behind this largesse. Miss Bassenthwaite had been told by Mr Andrew Drummond himself, the bank's then senior partner, when she had first received Miss Devenish into her establishment as a child a little under three years old, that her charge was an orphan, but that a sufficient sum had been deposited with the bank to pay for her education and keep in the first style.

By the time Harriet had grown old enough to wonder about the arrangements made for her, this Mr Drummond had died, but the money continued to arrive with the same punctual regularity as before.

In her early years at the school Harriet had been, to an extent, petted and spoiled by the other boarders who were all older than herself, as well as by the two teachers and servants, who were sorry for the mite. Miss Bassenthwaite herself treated Harriet as a daughter—or at least, as a well-loved niece. Having known nothing else, Harriet did not at first feel the lack of regular parents, and was a carefree, happy, loveable child.

By the time she was eight, Harriet shared the dormitory with five other little girls who formed the junior section of the small school which never had more than sixteen pupils all told. Having been an inmate of the school for so long, and not suffering in the least from shyness, Harriet was almost at once the leader in all kinds of pranks, from persuading Cook to let her have sugared almonds and macaroons and gingerbread for a midnight feast, to leading a party of her fellows to hunt for the ghost said to be haunting the old abbey ruins in the school grounds; and even on occasion, together with her particular friend, Blanche Sawston, pretending to be ghosts, draping themselves in their pillowslips, to the bewildered consternation of Jedediah, the gardener, who saw them once as he was returning from a visit to the Blue Boar in Carlisle, and who ever afterwards was careful never to approach the ruins after dark.

The scolding Harriet received on that occasion was as nothing to the time when she bought a white mouse from

Sam, the gardener's boy, and let it loose during·the embroidery lesson. Miss Pinkerton, the teacher, normally the quietest female imaginable, was terrified, and screamed and shrieked, and jumped up on a chair, and had to be restored with hartshorn drops, and not less than half a glass of Miss Bassenthwaite's best medicinal brandy.

But Miss Bassenthwaite could not remain angry for long, no matter what Harriet did, for she was such a laughing, sunny child, and apologized so prettily for the trouble and dismay she had caused, and had, indeed, so good a heart, being always ready to help wherever she could, that Miss Bassenthwaite rightly put down such escapades to childish naughtiness, and made no difference in her treatment of Harriet after the offence had been punished.

As for Harriet, though not in the least unhappy, it was only to be expected that she should wonder a good deal about her lost parents: who they had been and what they had been like. That they were both dead she had been told from the first: killed in a carriage accident. As she grew older, she questioned Miss Bassenthwaite more frequently about them, but Miss Bassenthwaite could tell her nothing, other than that the money came from the bank in London, which Harriet knew already, but with which she always had to be content.

Sometimes it occurred to her that is was not that Miss Bassenthwaite could not so much as that she would not tell her anything more; but as time went by, the girl came to believe that her teacher was as innocent as she professed, though she could not help but think it a pity that Miss Bassenthwaite had not been a deal more curious in the beginning.

As a result of the vacuum, Harriet was able to allow her imagination to wander unchecked. Her best dream was to imagine herself the daughter of some great man—very rich—perhaps a duke, and that her mother had died at her birth, and that her father, so much in love with his wife, had not been able to bear the sight of the child who was a constant reminder of his dead spouse, and so had sent her away. It was the sort of tragical, romantical idea that appealed very much to Harriet at one time.

At other times Harriet faced the fact, bravely, that her parents might have come from a very different walk of life, and that it might be much better for her to remain in ignorance of their identity. Suppose they should turn out to be not only base-born, but also malefactors—thieves, perhaps, or horse-stealers—or even—murderers! Really it would be exceedingly disagreeable to find oneself the daughter of such a one!

It was on these occasions that Harriet wavered in her intention of one day going to Drummonds and asking some pertinent questions about the origin of the money which kept her.

Her questionings grew greater as she grew older and met the families of fellow-pupils, being sometimes asked to stay with them during the holidays. The parents, particularly the mothers, very frequently displayed a good deal of curiosity as to Harriet's antecedents; but though Harriet was unable to dispel their curiosity, the liberal allowance provided for her was well known, and made her quite a fitting companion for their daughters.

She necessarily grew more conscious of her abandoned state: other girls could produce a mother and father, sisters, brothers, aunts, uncles, grandparents: Harriet had nothing. She never so much as received a letter. As a small child this had not worried her in the least; she had accepted her situation without question or concern. But as each birthday passed, though Harriet did not repine, she became aware of how different she was from the other children.

Matters came to a head when one day Harriet was taunted by a new child to Miss Bassenthwaite's Academy, one Susan Holt, who was jealous of Harriet for what she saw as her undoubtedly priviliged position in the school establishment. Harriet determined to do something about the matter, and after a good deal of cogitation, at last wrote a letter, slipping it into the mail before it was distributed, and professing profound surprise when it was handed to her by Miss Bassenthwaite.

As it happened, this was upon Harriet's thirteenth birthday. Harriet took the letter with shining eyes and opened it before her school-fellows and read it to herself with a great many 'Oohs' and 'Aahs' and 'Oh, nos!'

Such excitement was bound to have an effect upon her listeners, who begged Harriet to read her letter aloud, which Harriet did most willingly, describing with very dramatic voice and gesture the trials and dangers her guardian had endured in the war against Boney in the Peninsula. In the end, the letter was handed about amongst the girls, who all of them fell promptly in love with the writer, declaring him to be the bravest man in the world, and envying Harriet her luck in having such a guardian.

When Miss Bassenthwaite heard about the letter, naturally she questioned Harriet, who professed entire ignorance, but said that she was very glad her guardian had taken it into his head to recognize her at last. Miss Bassenthwaite remained somewhat concerned for some days, but to Harriet's relief seemed to forget about it quickly enough.

Harriet would have done no more in that line, but the girls so frequently asked her if she had heard again from her guardian, and so longed to hear from him, that when her fourteenth birthday came round, Harriet penned another letter to herself, which the girls begged Harriet to let them see. This she duly did, and felt quite proud of her composition as the girls sighed and exclaimed over the adventures and escapes of Harriet's mythical guardian which this time were more extraordinary than ever, and given in even greater detail.

After the letter on Harriet's fifteenth birthday, she actually wrote a reply which she addressed care of Lord Wellesley, the commander of the British troops in the Peninsula, to Lord Richard Halton, a colonel with His Lordship's army in Spain. She had chosen the name Halton from a nearby village in Cumberland, and the name Richard merely because she liked it. The Lord was an extra flourish, added partly because Harriet thought it sounded more romantic, and partly because Harriet thought it would serve Susan Holt right, for Miss Holt had been claiming precedence of all the other pupils on the grounds that her maternal grandfather was a viscount.

On her sixteenth birthday Harriet had the happiness of reading eyewitness' account of the Allies' entry into Paris at the end of March when Boney was beaten and sent off to exile on Elba. According to his letter, Lord Richard Halton played a vital part in the proceedings, and when Miss Susan Holt, more jealous than ever now due to the consequence gained by Harriet because of her brave and illustrious guardian, pointed out that Lord Richard was never mentioned in dispatches, Harriet pointed out scornfully that of course the commander-in-chief must take all the credit, but that everyone knew that the real work was done by the officers on the general's staff of which Lord Richard was the brightest ornament.

The seventeenth birthday letter came with news of Lord Richard's part in the Battle of Waterloo, on which Harriet expended more than usual thought and ingenuity, as well as some pocket money in buying the relevant newspapers.

'I have seen no mention of this Lord Richard Halton in my newspaper,' Miss Holt said loftily when Harriet had finished reading. 'I think it quite likely that he does not exist!'

'Not exist!' Harriet cried. 'And how would you know anything about the matter?'

'I have asked my mamma if she has heard of him, and she tells me that she has never head the name.'

'That is not surprising,' Harriet returned more top-loftily still. 'My guardian has been fighting with our troops for years. He has been in the Peninsula since nineteen hundred and eight when Lord Wellesley first went there. He has not been in society at all!'

'He must have been very young when first he went abroad then,' Miss Holt said with deceptive nonchalance.

'Of course he was!' Harriet cried with injudicious vehemence. 'He is the bravest of the brave! As soon as he was able, he went to the continent to fight against Boney!'

'How old is he now, then?' Miss Holt enquired silkily.

'Oh, about—twenty-seven or eight, I do not know exactly,' Harriet returned snatching an age out of the air. After all, she had invented her guardian she could make him exactly as she wished. She had already said that he was tall and very handsome. Now she gave him what she thought was a very good age—not too old, and not too young.

'Really!' Miss Hold drawled, the light of scorn flashing in her eyes. 'I suppose then that he was made your guardian when still a schoolboy!'

For a second Harriet was taken aback, but she recovered the next moment. 'Of course not, silly!' she laughed. 'His father was my guardian, but when his father died, naturally I became his son's ward.'

'And just who is this Lord Richard Halton's father?' Miss Holt sneered.

'He was a duke, of course,' Harriet returned, herself scornful now. 'Anyone would know that a *Lord* Richard must be the son of a duke or a marquis.'

'But *which* duke?'

'If you look it up in Debrett, you will see for yourself!' Harriet answered rashly.

'I suppose his brother is the duke now?' sneered Miss Holt.

'Of course he is!' Harriet returned, feeling vexed that she had not been modest enough to keep her guardian a plain mister, and so avoid all these complications. But luckily Susan Holt, older than Harriet, was expected to leave the school shortly; she would then be rid of these awkward questions, and it would not matter a button if Susan could not find Lord Richard Halton in the work of reference.

And if the worst came to the worst, Harriet could always kill off her guardian.

Susan Holt was to make her come-out in London, and gave herself a good many airs because of it. Harriet joined with the other less fortunate girls who did not expect to make their curtsy to the Regent, speculating on what it would be like to do the season.

'But surely, Harriet, your guardian will have you brought out!' her particular friend Blanche asked once when they were alone together. 'After all, the brother of a duke . . . !'

'I do not know, Blanche, my guardian has said nothing of it,' Harriet answered, considering the advisability of writing herself a letter in which such plans were put forward.

But before she got round to doing it, Susan Holt left; and shortly two other girls with whom she had grown up; and lastly Blanche Sawstone herself. Harriet did feel very lonely then, wondering what was going to happen to her, and having to make more frequent explanations to the remaining girls to account for her guardian's non-appearance. After all, the war was over now; there was really nothing to keep him away. Harriet wrote herself a letter then, in which Lord Richard explained that he was part of the army of occupation, and would be returning to England when he could.

This served to stave off questions for a while, but when in the spring of 1816 Harriet received a letter from Blanche Sawston, inviting her for a long visit, Harriet read pity in between the lines and declined the invitation, though Miss Bassenthwaite urged her to accept it.

'But—supposing I were away and my guardian came for me!' Harriet cried. 'It would be too awful!'

'I suppose you are right, my dear,' Miss Bassenthwaite said doubtfully. 'But I do wish we might hear something definite as to your future. You will be eighteen this summer. I think I will write again to Drummond's to ask what plans have been made for your future. I will tell them that you have learnt all that the school can teach you, and that you are prepared in every particular to take your place in the wider world. But I do think it odd that your guardian says nothing.'

'Would you like me to draft a letter for you, ma'am?' Harriet asked quickly, fearful that Miss Bassenthwaite might mention the mythical guardian, and to this Miss Bassenthwaite agreed.

A careful letter was sent therefore, but all the reply that came from the bank was that Miss Devenish was to remain some time longer at the academy, and that Miss Bassenthwaite would be informed of how she should proceed in due course.

Thoroughly unsettled, Harriet determined that she would have to go to London herself; it was impossible to find out anything at this distance, but if she herself explained her circumstances to the bank, then surely something would be done. Accordingly, therefore, she prepared a letter from her guardian to Miss Bassenthwaite, instructing that Miss Devenish was to be sent post to London, as it was impossible for Lord Richard to come to Cumberland, and meaning to put it with the other mail when opportunity offered.

She had the letter in her possession still when, to her complete astonishment, she was summoned to Miss Bassenthwaite's salon, and was there presented to a tall, dark, very handsome and most distinguished stranger.

'My dear Harriet,' Miss Bassenthwaite beamed, 'such a surprise! Allow me to introduce you to your guardian, Lord Richard Halton. This is your ward, Lord Richard. I hope you will think that we have brought her up in accordance with your instructions?'

The man ran an appraising eye over Harriet as she curtsied, then he took her hand and kissed her cheek. 'I am glad to see you again at last, my dear,' he smiled. 'You are much prettier than I remember you—Harriet. You were not blessed with much hair then, of course,' the man went on. 'It must be, let me see, fifteen years or so ago?'

Harriet stared at the man whose grey eyes were laughing at her. 'I-I am afraid I do not remember sir!' she gulped.

'Of course not! You were a tiny child then!' Lord Richard now said kindly.

'Yes, indeed,' Miss Bassenthwaite sighed; 'Harriet has been here since before she was three. We shall be sorry to lose her, Lord Richard; she is a dear, sweet girl,' And Miss Bassenthwaite wiped her eyes, and caught hold of Harriet's hand fondly.

'I am delighted to hear that, ma'am,' the man calling himself Lord Richard returned with an approving glance at the girl. His face broke into a grin as he regarded Harriet. 'I have often wondered what my little ward was like now!'

'Ah, yes; the wars, my lord!' Miss Bassenthwaite sighed. 'They have been responsible for a deal of hardship.'

'Indeed they have, ma'am!'

The conversation was continued between the two, Miss Bassenthwaite recalling incidents of Harriet's career at school, and Lord Richard encouraging her to reveal more, while Harriet struggled to regain her composure, trying to decide who the man could possibly be and why he had come to meet her. For though he said everything that he should to Miss Bassenthwaite, Harriet could not rid her mind of the certainty that the man was an impostor. There was something too conspiratorial in his glance when he looked at her for him to be genuine. But that she had never seen him before she was quite certain.

But then Miss Bassenthwaite was called away to deal with some domestic matter, and she excused herself, saying, 'I dare say you will like to get to know your ward again, Lord Richard. If you will excuse me, I will leave you for a while, and afterwards, I hope you will do me the honour of dining here?'

'That is very kind, ma'am, but I am anxious to return to London as soon as possible.'

'Oh!' Miss Bassenthwaite looked very disappointed, but deferred to the gentlemen's wishes. 'Oh, dear. What a pity!

But in that case I must see that Harriet's things are packed and ready.' And with that she departed, beaming at them as she closed the door.

Harriet had remained unusually silent up to now. Now she turned to stare at the man, her head still in a whirl, but determined to find out the truth.

'Well, sir?' Harriet demanded in a low voice; 'Who are you?

'Lord Richard Halton, at your service, ma'am.' And the man bowed.

'Lord Richard—! Pray do not pretend to me, sir. What is your real name?'

'Richard Halton,' the man repeated with a grin. 'And has been from my birth, I promise you.'

'Can you prove it?'

'My servant at the inn will vouch for me.'

'That would mean nothing! He might be persuaded—bribed—to say anything!'

The man calling himself Lord Richard thought for a moment, then produced a watch from his pocket and opened the back. 'I have this, Miss Devenish, given to me upon my eighteenth birthday. And this.' Here the man pulled a snuff-box from his pocket and snapped open its lid also. Then he held out the two items to Harriet.

She took them and read the inscriptions which both named their owner as Richard Halton.

'And how am I to know that you have not stolen these, sir?'

'I assure you, I am not in the habit of purloining things, Miss Devenish. Happily, I have no need to do so,' the man added with a grin.

For some reason, Harriet believed this, and felt herself blushing. 'I beg your pardon, sir, but—well, you must ad-

12

mit that it really is odd that you come here, claiming to be my guardian when having had none, I had to make up one—!'

'Ah, I see now! You happened to make up my name for your—mythical protector?'

Harriet nodded.

'I am vastly intrigued, Miss Devenish, that you lighted on my own name. But, pray tell me, why all this was necessary.' Lord Richard grinned again. 'After all, ma'am, it is not every day that a man finds himself the guardian of a delightful and exceedingly pretty young woman!'

Harriet could not help blushing again, but she smiled also. She felt suddenly that she could trust him. So she explained about her orphaned state, and how, in the end, she had been driven to write letters to him and eventually to herself. 'They were very *good* letters, I promise you, my lord. You would not have been at all ashamed of them. The other girls loved them, and could hardly wait until the next one came. But you wrote only once a year—for my birthday.

'I see. Er-how many letters did I write to you?'

'The first arrived on my thirteenth birthday—and there has been one a year since then.'

'That makes-er-four?'

'No, five. But you did write one other to let me know that you would not be coming home immediately after Waterloo. So I have six in all.'

'I see. And-er-where have I been since your thirteenth birthday?'

'Fighting Boney, of course! You were on Wellesley's staff. You were very brave.'

'Was I? I am glad to hear it. Pray tell me more.'

'Well, you sailed to Portugal and landed at Lisbon with

13

Wellesley. You were with him when he crossed the Douro; you personally helped to bring over one of the wine-barges, although Soult's scouts fired on you, and missed your head by less than a sixteenth of an inch! In fact, you had a furrow through your hair to show where it had passed. But happily, you were not wounded!'

'I am delighted to hear it!'

'And after you shared with Wellesley the dinner that had been cooked for Marshal Soult. You found it delicious, and said it was the best meal you had had in days! You are quite fond of your food, you know!'

'Well, you know that an army is supposed to march on its belly! What else did I do? I am vastly intrigued to hear!'

'I tell you, you were tremendously brave! You were with Wellesley continually. At Talavera you were nearly captured when you rushed before the enemy to save a wounded English corporal. You gave him the last drop of water from your flask, though you were nearly dead with thirst yourself. And the following morning you were with the Forty-Eighth when the Frenchies scaled the Cerro de Medellin, and you shot down a hundred of them yourself! And when you had no more shot, you took out your sabre and cut down a hundred more!'

'Did I? I seem to have done very valiantly. Tell me, was I Foot or Cavalry?'

'Both!' Harriet cried dramatically. 'When you had a horse you fought like a god. And when your horse was shot under you, you fought on foot like a demon! Either way, no Frenchie in your path stood a chance!' Harriet's eyes were now shining with excitement.

'A life full of incident! Pray tell me more!'

'It was always the same. You were always in the vanguard—the bravest of the brave! At Busaco, at Almeida, at Albuera, at Cuidad Rodrigo, at Vittoria—'

'And I wrote to you of these battles?'

'Oh, yes! Directly afterwards.'

'And saved them for your birthdays?'

'Yes. You see, you could not always send the letters directly. I looked forward to receiving your letters very much, you know. And so did all the girls.'

'Just as I looked forward to receiving yours, my dear Miss Devenish.'

'You mean—my letters did reach you!' Harriet cried amazed.

'Of course. How else should I be here? Frequently, of course, they did not catch up with me till months after you had sent them. The first one reached me, I recall, as we were fighting for San Sebastian.'

'Ah! You were very brave there also!'

'Yes, I think I was.'

Harriet stared at Lord Richard. 'Were you really—at San Sebastian?'

''Indeed I was! I remember it very well!'

'Were you—by and chance—at Victoria?'

'I was there also.'

'And Cuidad Rodrigo—and Albuera—and Almeida—and Busaco?'

Lord Richard nodded.

'And—and did you go to the Peninsula with Wellesley?'

'Ah, well—no; not exactly.'

'Not!'

'No. I was already at Lisbon to meet Wellesley. I had been in Spain before, you see—I went out first with Sir Harry Burrard.'

'Oh! I-I must have misunderstood that!'

15

'It would be easy to do,' Lord Richard said comfortingly. 'Things were very confused.'

'But—you received my letters!'

'Oh, yes! The next one I received, I recollect, came while I was in Paris.'

'That was a most exciting time for you! You were *very* popular!'

'How did you know that! And your third letter reached me there also—after Waterloo.'

'Oh, I am so glad you were there! I should not like to have been wrong in that. You saved a whole troop at Waterloo, you know.'

'I did?'

Harriet nodded. 'I am so glad you exist, my lord!' She smiled. 'It is really very gratifying! To have been right about you, I mean!'

'I must say, I do regret it greatly, Miss Devenish, that I am not indeed your guardian.'

The girl laughed. 'And I, my lord! But tell me, why *did* you come to see me?'

'Curiosity, Miss Devenish,' Lord Richard answered promptly. 'There I was, receiving suddenly letters from a completely unknown young lady who called me her guardian—most amusing and—and literate letters, I must say. Of course I was curious to meet such a creature.'

'And-and you approve, my lord?' Harriet asked archly.

'Indeed, I do, ma'am!'

'Then—' Harriet paused and took a deep breath, 'then—play the part of my guardian, my lord! Take me to London with you, I beg you!'

'My dear young lady, what are you asking!'

'Miss Bassenthwaite is having my valises packed now!

I shall be ready to go with you directly!' Harriet urged recklessly.

'But, Miss Devenish—I am *not* your guardian!' Lord Richard spoke gravely now. 'I am but a figment of your imagination!'

'Oh, I know that, my lord! And I promise not to be any burden to you, truly! But—I must go to London. I have been meaning to go very shortly for some time! You see, I think I have not mentioned—Miss Bassenthwaite very regularly—every month—receives money for my keep from Drummond's Bank in London. Who pays this money or where it comes from she does not know. It is a most generous sum that comes, but—well, I am nearly eighteen, and I can not remain at school much longer, and I want to know if anything is planned for me—if this unknown benefactor means to cut me off now, or if I may continue to expect an allowance. Letters have told us nothing, and I want to go to the bank to find out for myself. And as you are going to London, it would be exceedingly convenient!' Harried finished, rather breathless.

'But, Miss Devenish, you must see that it would not be at all proper for you to travel throughout the length of England alone with me. Your reputation would be in shreds!'

'But—not if you were my guardian! Besides, we would be traveling in quite the opposite direction from Gretna Green!'

'That has nothing to do with it!'

'Well, nobody would think that you were eloping with me, would they?' Harriet asked reasonably. 'I could travel as your ward, and no-one would think any the worse of either of us!'

'But it is not true! You are not my ward!'

'But everything else is true! It would be only a tiny pretence!'

'Miss Devenish! I would not dream of doing anything so shatter-brained as making off to London with you!'

'But I mean to go to London in any case'! If I do not go with you, my guardian is to send Miss Bassenthwaite a letter saying that he wishes me to come to London as he is unable to come for me. I can show you the letter if you like!'

'I'll wager you can!'

'I will just go and get it!'

'No, Miss Devenish! No! It is quite impossible!' Lord Richard sounded quite desperate now, as if he were caught in a nightmare and knew not how to extricate himself.

'Oh, *please*, Lord Richard! Please! *Please!*' And Harriet flung herself on her knees and clutched one of Lord Richard's hands. 'I will be as quiet as a mouse and not trouble you with constant chatter, and I have some money saved! I will be able to pay for my food! I shall not be the least trouble to you, I promise! And—I know I should be safe with you!'

Lord Richard pulled his hand away. 'No, Miss Devenish! I am sorry, but—no! And—please do get up, you nonsensical child!'

Harriet stared up at him for a moment, and large tears welled in her big blue eyes. 'I think you are quite horrid!' she cried, scrambling to her feet. 'I do not like you at all!'

'I am very sorry for that, Miss Devenish, for I like you very much.'

'Well, then—why will not you help me?'

'Consider, Miss Devenish, how old are you? Sixteen?'

'Seventeen! Nearly Eighteen!'

'Until a short time ago, you have never seen me! Just

18

think! An unknown man taking an unknown woman on such a journey! It would be the height of folly! Why! I might be arrested for abducting you!'

'But I have no kin!'

'Somebody pays for you here!'

'And all I want is to find out who it is! I am only asking you to take me to London!'

'You know nothing about me, Miss Devenish! I might be the most terrible rake: have the most appalling reputation! And it is certain that *you* would have none when we arrive in London!'

'I tell you I trust you! And—no-one need know anything about it. You could drop me at Drummond's Bank, and the clerk who sends the drafts—Mr. Bacup—would help me, I am sure.'

'I doubt that any clerk would be in any position to help you.'

'Oh, please, Lord Richard!' Harriet smiled brokenly in a manner which she knew was very appealing. For a moment she saw a shadow of indecision in the man's face, and she made her lower lip tremble piteously.

But Lord Richard hardened his heart. 'No, Miss Devenish! Positively no! I would be a veritable gabey to get myself caught up in such a schoolgirl scrape!' And he rose and walked a hurried pace or two up and down.

'I am not a schoolgirl! And I will *pay* you if you wish!' The man turned to face her. 'And if you did not mean to take me for your ward,' Harriet went on hotly, 'I do not see why you bothered to come here at all!'

'Believe me, Miss Devenish, I am beginning to wish that I had not! It was madness in me to act on the spur of the moment, and I regret very much that my curiosity got the better of my sense!'

19

'And what am I going to say to Miss Bassenthwaite when she asks me where you are gone? You can not desert me like this!'

'I have no doubt, Miss Devenish, that your fertile brain will think up some perfectly logical explanation. If you can persuade Miss Bassenthwaite that a mythical guardian exists, then you can persuade her of anything! Clearly you have an excess of imagination, and I dare swear that it will not let you down now! Goodbye, Miss Devenish! It has been a pleasure meeting you, but—I should never have come. Pray, make my excuses to Miss Bassenthwaite.'

And with that, Lord Richard bowed hurriedly and went hastily through the door.

'Oh! Come back! Come back!' Harriet shrieked, and ran two or three steps towards the door. But then she stopped. After all, what right had she to expect Lord Richard to help her? That she had lighted on the name of a real man for her imaginary guardian was the merest chance, and gave her no claim on the living man.

On the other hand, he *had* sought her out, and introduced himself to Miss Bassenthwaite as her guardian, and so had turned the chimera into a real man.

She stood pondering for a few moments, and in the end convinced herself that Lord Richard Halton did at the least owe her help in reaching London. Determinedly then, she went to see how her packing was proceeding, and found Miss Bassenthwaite with two of the maids, putting the last of her clothes into a small portmanteau.

'Oh, Miss Bassenthwaite,' Harriet began blithely, crossing her fingers behind her back, 'my guardian has left to return to the inn. You remember he said that he was in a hurry to return to London. He sends you his apologies for departing so, and asked if my luggage may be sent to him at the inn where I am to meet him, for he is determined to set off tonight.

'Oh, my dear Harriet!' Miss Bassenthwaite wailed, 'this is so sudden! I had hoped that Lord Richard would stay.'

'He sent you a thousand apologies, ma'am, but—time is very pressing.'

Miss Bassenthwaite, who had little experience of men except as the fathers of her pupils, was always prepared to defer to the whims and requirements of the stronger sex. Now she accepted without further question that Lord Richard had urgent business on hand, and that Harriet and her luggage must be conveyed after him.

'Very well, my dear,' she said briskly. 'If you must go at once, you must go. But I am sorry to be losing you after all these years.'

Harriet had been putting on her bonnet and buttoning her pelisse. Now it came to her as Miss Bassenthwaite spoke that she was to leave everything she had hitherto known and loved. Impulsively, she flung her arms about Miss Bassenthwaite. 'Oh, I shall see you again, dear ma'am. This does not mean that we shall never meet again! How could I lose you, after all your kindnesses to me?'

Miss Bassenthwaite was equally affected, and for some moments the two clung to each other weeping. It was Miss Bassenthwaite who pulled herself together first.

'Well, my dear, you must not keep his lordship waiting. Men are very particular about punctuality, I know. And I am sure you will conduct yourself as becomes a pupil of my academy, Harriet. Always remember what we have taught you. There, now, dry your eyes, my dear, and let me see the smile I know so well.'

Harriet essayed a tremulous smile.

'That is much better, my dear. Now, to which inn must Joshua convey you?'

Harriet stared non-plussed. She had not the least idea where Lord Richard might have put up.

'Well, I dare say it will be the White Hart,' Miss Bassenthwaite said comfortably. 'It is quite the best inn for a gentlemen of quality. And if by chance Lord Richard should not be there, Joshua may take you to the George or look elsewhere till you find your guardian.'

Harriet said hurried goodbyes to the remaining pupils in the school and to the teachers and the domestics, while Joshua harnessed the carriage. Her heart was still heavy as she climbed up beside the man in the little low phaeton which Miss Bassenthwaite used for local journeys. She turned to wave goodbye as Joshua urged the pony to a gentle trot down the drive, acutely conscious that she was leaving the safety of Miss Bassenthwaite's academy, and that her schoolgirl days were ended at last.

Two

As the little carriage proceeded down the drive, and Miss Bassenthwaite was lost to sight, Harriet dried her tears, and began to plan more exactly what she should do. And if she failed to persuade Lord Richard to take her with him, well, she could catch the London coach as she had originally intended, the fare for which she had been saving out of her pocket money for the past year.

They reached the White Hart in the town, and Joshua was dispatched into the inn to find out if Lord Richard Halton were there. The man returned with the news that Lord Richard was indeed inside, and at the moment engaged in consuming a hearty dinner, though it was expected that he would depart very shortly. Joshua pointed across the busy yard to a travelling chaise backed under a sheltering roof. 'I collect that that is his lordship's carriage, Miss.'

'In that case, please to put my valise and portmanteau beside it Joshua, ready to be loaded.'

This done, Harriet said goodbye to the old man, and gave him as big a vail as she could afford, and was about to proceed into the inn to seek out Lord Richard, when she noticed ostlers bringing horses up to Lord Richard's carriage.

A much better idea then occurred to her. Remembering Lord Richard's decided disinclination to take her with him, suppose she hid herself in the chaise! If she were not discovered till they were well outside Carlisle, Lord Richard would hardly be so cruel as to dump her down in the countryside, but might well continue with her to London.

Accordingly, Harriet went over to the carriage, and while the ostlers were occupied in putting the horses to, she opened the carriage door on the side away from the inn entrance, and heaved her valise and portmanteau onto the floor of the carriage and pushed them under the seat.

Her first idea had been that she should hide under the seat also, but although her portmanteau was only a small one, as was her valise, when they were in place, there was no room for Harriet's person as well.

After an unsuccessful attempt, Harriet clambered to the ground again and looked about her anxiously, wondering where she could possible conceal herself now. Had it been a public vehicle, she might have gone in the basket behind, but of course there was no such item on this carriage. There was however, a big trunk behind, and Harriet eyed it hopefully. Glancing about her surreptitiously to make sure she was not observed she tugged at the straps fastening the trunk. A quick lift of the lid and a peep inside showed a nearly empty receptacle. A few items of clothing only lay at the bottom, and there was more than enough room to accommodate herself.

Following another swift glance about her, Harriet, without a moment's hesitation, scrambled into the trunk and pulled the lid down upon herself. She twisted and turned to get herself comfortable, and found that the clothes at the bottom of the trunk made quite a soft bed. It was somewhat stuffy inside the trunk, but that was the greatest discomfort; but she hoped that Lord Richard would not be long in starting.

There had been a good deal of noise in the inn yard where carriages were constantly entering and departing, but now to Harriet such noise was muffled. She ventured to raise the lid of the trunk an inch or two to look out, but she could see only the walls of the open coach-house; and it took her such a long time to get herself comfortable again, that she did not bother to raise the lid a second time, but settled down to wait for Lord Richard's departure.

She had not the least recollection where she was when first she woke. All around her was warm, black stuffiness, and she was being shaken gently. From somewhere near at hand came the sound of trotting horses, but it was only after a few moments that Harriet realized that they were causing the jolting she felt, and she remembered where she was. Gingerly she stretched up an arm and pushed against the lid of the trunk.

She was able to raise it a bare inch. She understood then that the straps must have been rebuckled, and felt some consternation at the realization that she was unable to get out of the trunk. Holding the lid open, she breathed in refreshing drafts of clean, cool air.

But soon her arm began to ache, and the girl scrambled to her knees, and she peered through the crack, keeping the lid raised by supporting it against her head.

Dusk was falling, but there was light enough still to see that they were travelling along a country road with hedges on each side, dark against the faint paleness lingering in the sky. Clearly they were well out of Carlisle, and Harriet considered calling to the coachman to attract his attention.

But then it came to her that they could not be so very far from Carlisle yet, and if Lord Richard knew of her presence so soon, he might well turn round and take her back to Miss Bassenthwaite's. And that Harriet could not bear. So she remained where she was, crouching in the trunk, till she felt pins and needles in her legs, and was forced to lie down again and rub her limbs till feeling returned to them. She would wait, she decided, till they came to an inn and stopped to change the horses.

Because of the stuffiness, Harriet was forced often to kneel up and breath in the fresh night air; then the strain on her back became so painful that she was forced to lie down again. It was during one of these periods when she was lying with closed eyes, that she heard different sounds outside the trunk. They had passed several other travellers on the road, but there was something different about this noise, a sort of muffled scuffling. Scrambling onto her knees, Harriet pushed up the lid just in time to hear a rough voice shouting at them to halt.

Alert at once, Harriet stiffened with fear, for she knew what such an encounter must mean! One of the highwaymen must now have seized the horses for the chaise halted with a jerk, and Harriet was pitched against the side of the trunk with such force that it brought tears to her eyes. Then she was flung against the other side of the trunk, bruising elbows and knees in different places, as one of the horses obviously succeded in rearing. Her first thought now was regret for her rashness in choosing such a hiding place.

A second later she feared for her life. A shot rang out, followed by further shouts. Scufflings and oaths came to her clearly as she cowered in the trunk, wondering what was happening. Another shot followed the first, to be succeeded by the sounds of horses' hooves thudding away over turf. Then the coach door was flung open and yet another shot burst through the night. There came the sound of boots landing on the road, and Lord Richard's voice cried out, 'Are you all right, Porter?'

'All well, my lord,' came the reply. 'I think you winged one o' them!'

'Then I trust we shall not be troubled by them again!'

Harriet's own voice broke out then. 'Help! My lord, help!'

Her voice made little impact, but both men heard it, and were abruptly silent.

Harriet called again, 'Let me out, please, my lord!'

'Who are you? Where are you?' Lord Richard demanded.

'I am here! In the trunk!' Harriet cried weakly, her bruises beginning to throb most painfully now.

There came the brisk sound of boots approaching the rear of the carriage. The next moment the straps were unbuckled and the lid flung up. Harriet saw a dark shape towering over her, holding what looked horridly like a pistol.

She gave a little scream, and knelt up.

'Who are you? What are you doing hiding there?' Lord Richard demanded, aiming the pistol at her.

The coachman joined his master now, carrying one of the carriage lanterns, and Harriet was revealed in all her dishevelment.

'Miss Devenish!' Lord Richard gasped. 'What in thunder are you doing in my trunk?'

'I-I wanted to get to London, my lord!' Harriet gasped piteously.

'You-you—nonsensical child!' Lord Richard burst out wrathfully, words nearly failing him.

27

Tears began to run down Harriet's cheeks. 'But—you wouldn't take me! And—Miss B-Bassenthwaite had packed all my things, and I could not tell her that you were gone off without me. She-she thought you were such a gentleman!' Harriet added reproachfully.

Lord Richard continued to stare at Harriet for some moments, without reply. The he said abruptly to Porter, 'How far are we from Carlisle?'

'Nigh forty miles, my lord. We should reach Kendal in ten miles or so.'

The master appeared to consider this, and Harriet quavered, 'You are not going to leave me here, are you, my lord?'

'Of course not! What do you think I am? I shall take you on to Kendal, then pack you off back to Carlisle on the first coach.'

'But I want to go to London! I am too old to remain at school any longer!' Harriet wailed.

'Oh, for heaven's sake do not weep! I can not abide a weeping woman! Here; give me your hand.'

Harriet did her best to blink back her tears. She rarely wept, but what with the bruises and the fright she had had, and now being told that Lord Richard was bent on sending her back to Carlisle was too much for her.

Seated a few minutes later in the chaise beside Lord Richard, she sniffed once or twice. Silently her companion proffered a handkerchief, and with a muffled 'Thank you' Harriet blew her nose loudly, and felt much better—at least for the moment. But then she was conscious again of her bruises throbbing, and in addition, she felt distinctly hungry.

She swallowed to control her breath, then said in as

bright a voice as she could manage, 'Only a few more miles to Kendal I think your coachman said, my lord?'

'Yes.'

'I am so glad. I am very hungry.'

'Serve you right!' came the heartless reply. 'I've never heard of such a hare-brained scheme in my life!'

'If you had agreed to take me in the normal way, I should not have been put to these shifts!' Harriet retorted. 'I must say, looking at it dispassionately, it really does seem all your fault, my lord!'

'Does it indeed!'

'Yes, it does!' Harriet cried, warming to her theme. 'Had you not come to Miss Bassenthwaite's, I should never have known of your existence. But as you did appear there, *and* fit almost to the letter with all that I had told of you, I do think it very unreasonable in you to expect to go away again and leave me quite flat! I think you do owe me something! All I want is for you to take me to London. Once there, I shall quite be able to look after myself.'

'Oh! And what do you propose to do?'

'I have told you. I shall go to Drummond's to find out if my allowance will continue. If it does, there will be no problem. If not—then—then I shall find a position—as a governess—or a companion.'

'You! A governess!' Lord Richard jeered.

'I can speak Italian, *and* play the harp—as well as all the usual things!'

'Can you indeed! Then it is a pity your commonsense was not so well developed!'

'Oh!' Harriet flounced round to look out of the window. In so doing she banged one bruised elbow on the window frame, but managed to stifle a yelp. She sat up very straight and dignified.

'My dear young lady,' Lord Richard now said in quite a kind, reasonable voice, 'you must see that it is not at all the thing for you to be wandering about London quite without protection!'

'But what else am I to do? I can not remain at school for ever! I am nearly eighteen!'

'A great age!'

'Yes, it is! For a schoolgirl!'

At length Lord Richard had to admit that he saw the justice of this, but still maintained that it was his duty to send her back to Carlisle.

'But it will be quite useless,' Harriet said frankly. 'For when the stage stopped again, I should leave it, and take the next coach to London.'

The remainder of the distance to Kendal was passed in variations of this conversation; Harriet insisting that she would go to London by hook or by crook, and Lord Richard anxious to wash his hands of her, but feeling some responsibility for her in spite of himself.

At Kendal they dined together, and Lord Richard enquired the time of the next coach to Carlisle. Harriet's eyes sparkled as she heard the manner in which he did this. They sparkled even more when the inn-keeper replied that the next coach to the Border did not depart until the next day, one having just left.

'You called me your ward!' Harriet gloated when they were alone again.

'And how else am I to explain what you are doing with me, you troublesome creature?'

'Oh! I do not mind in the least!' Harriet returned airily.

'And now I suppose I must remain here till morning to see you safely on the Carlisle coach?'

'I tell you, my lord, I shall go to London, whether you take me or no!'

Lord Richard stared gloomily into the fire. Harriet watched him, a feeling of triumph growing within her. She thought she had won at last.

She was not mistaken. Lord Richard said after a while, accompanying his words with no friendly look, 'Very well. I must suppose that you will be safer with me than gallivanting about England alone. I must tell you, Miss Devenish, that I hold no very high opinion of your conduct or your sense, but I must suppose myself even less a creature of sense to get myself involved with you. I will take you to London, and you will travel as if you were indeed my ward. And I expect you to give me the obedience—and respect—due to such a relationship.'

Harriet could not restrain a giggle at this, and Lord Richard eyed her severely. He continued sternly, 'When we get to London, I shall find suitable, respectable lodgings for you, and I expect you to remain there until some other suitable arrangement is made for you. Do you promise this?'

'Oh, yes, my lord! I promise that willingly.' Having got her own way, Harriet was all smiles and perfectly amenable. As their journey continued, Harriet regained all her wonted good spirits and amiability, and chattered away about life at Miss Bassenthwaite's in such an amusing fashion, that Lord Richard found that the tedious journey to the south passed very agreeably. And if from time to time he had a suspicion, based on his previous knowledge of the use Harriet made of her oversized imagination, that some of the stories Harriet regaled him with and which he found so diverting, were embroidered and bespangled out of all recognition, he made no protest, but allowed himself to be entertained.

The result of all this was that at the end of the journey they arrived in London in the best of good spirits and in perfect charity with one another. At each inn where they had spent a night upon the road, Harriet had been named as his lordship's ward, and by the end of the journey, Harriet at least felt that it could well be so.

She felt that she had chosen her guardian well. Lord Richard was both handsome and noble, and also plainly, very rich; he was accorded deference wherever they stopped. In battle he had been as brave and courageous in the face of the enemy as she had imagined her mythical guardian; and, now that the first difficulties were over he was kind and solicitous, and very willing to be agreeable and laugh at Harriet's tales. Harriet had quite forgiven him for his first stuffiness. After all, she reminded herself, it had been occasioned on her own account; and, as he was not so very young now, it was only natural that he should be a little prudish.

What his lordship thought of Harriet, the girl could only guess, but she was quite certain that he liked her now: she could see it in his eyes and the way in which he smiled at her.

As they clattered into London Harriet looked about her excitedly. If on her occasional visits into Carlisle she had thought that a busy place, it was as nothing compared with London, where the endless streets were all thronged and noisy with horses and carriages and the cries of muffin-men and flower-sellers and milkmen and a hundred other pedlars, as well as the press of so many pedestrians and the ceaseless chink of pattens on the cobbles.

Reaching the fashionable West End Harriet was all agog,

gazing out at the elegant shops and modish people, her eyes almost popping out of her head as she saw such sights as she had never dreamt of in the north. Lord Richard watched her, amused by her excited squeaks and gasps.

'Oh, pray look, my lord! Did ever you see such a quiz of a bonnet?' Harriet cried, pointing out a woman whose face was entirely hidden by her poke, which stretched a good foot above her head. 'And just see how she carries herself!'

'My dear Miss Devenish,' Lord Richard said, following her look, 'you will soon grow used to that sort of thing. That creature is in the height of fashion here.

'But she looks deformed!'

'That style of carriage is known as the Grecian bend.'

'Indeed! Then I prefer to remain English, my lord!'

'She gets that line by a little bolster tied to her waist at the back.'

'Really! Well, I can not think that I should ever want to look such a fright!'

Lord Richard smiled broadly. 'I wager, Miss Devenish, that if you remain a month in London, you will appear in something of that style yourself!'

'Never, my lord! It is not at all pretty!'

'Prettiness has little enough to do with fashion, Miss Devenish.'

Harriet looked at his lordship doubtfully, then turned back to watch the lively street scene.

They stopped at last outside a broad terrace house in a pleasant square shaded by trees. Harriet peered out of the window with great interest. 'Is this where you live, my lord?'

'No, Miss Devenish, I do not. But it is the home of the lady with whom I hope you may be able to stay.'

'It looks a very elegant house to be a lodging house, my lord!'

Lord Richard seemed to have some little difficulty in clearing his throat at that. 'It is not-er-a lodging house in the normal way of things, but—on this occasion,' he got out at last. He did not finish the sentence but opened the door and jumped down into the street. Porter appeared to let down the step, and Lord Richard handed Harriet out. She looked up at the house again, noting the elegant railings and the window boxes already bright with scarlet flowers. In the north, she remembered, the trees were only just breaking into leaf.

But she had not time for a long scrutiny, for Lord Richard took her arm, and hurried her up the steps and rang the bell.

The door was opened almost immediately by an aged servant whose face was transformed by a beam as soon as he saw Lord Richard. 'Oh, my lord, we are delighted to see you again. Her Grace was quite anxious at your sudden departure, and Lady Charlotte has called upon Her Grace several times.' The old eyes wavered to Harriet for a moment, then quickly looked back at Lord Richard. 'I will inform Her Grace at once of your arrival.

'Thank you, Carruthers.'

Once more the servant's eyes flickered to Harriet before the man turned and led the way into a small salon. The door was then closed upon Lord Richard and Harriet and the old man's footsteps were heard moving slowly across the marble-floored hall.

Harriet looked at Lord Richard 'Her—Grace?' she said quietly.

Lord Richard nodded.

'Your—mother?'

Lord Richard nodded again.

'Oh!' Harriet digested this. 'You mean,' she went on after a few moments, 'You—wish me to stay here with your mother, the duchess?'

'Precisely. Though first, of course, I must ask my mother if she is willing.'

'Of course!' Harriet looked very grave. 'I have never spoken to a duchess before,' she remarked after a moment.

'This duchess is not at all an ogre. She is a dowager duchess, of course.'

Harriet nodded. 'I did not for one moment think that your mother—that the duchess—would be so very—terrifying.' Suddenly she giggled. 'Oh! If only Susan Holt could see me now!'

'And who is Susan Holt?'

'I told you about her. She positively refused to believe that you existed! She said that I was making you up! Oh, she would be so jealous! Her mother is the daughter of a viscount, you see, so I had to make you a lord!'

'Oh course!' Lord Richard's eyes crinkled with amusement.

'And I am quite certain that Susan has never met a duchess!'

'Perhaps you may meet her in London, and then you could inform her of your superiority in that matter.'

Harriet grinned suddenly, but before she could reply the door opened and Carruthers stood there. 'Her Grace will be delighted to see you at once, my lord.'

'Thank you, Carruthers.' Lord Richard turned to Harriet. 'Will you excuse me for a few moments, Miss Devenish? I feel that I must-er-warn my mother first. As you will understand, the very last thing she is expecting me to have with me is-er-a ward.'

Harriet saw Carruthers' eyebrows rise. She said very demurely, 'Of course; I quite understand, my lord.'

While she sat alone waiting, Harriet had cause to feel pleased with her situation. She had achieved her first object—that of coming to London—and in some style. Now she was likely to be taken under the wing of a real duchess. With friends like a duchess and Lord Richard, surely she would soon find out from Drummond's what, if anything, her unknown benefactor proposed to do for her.

After a short time Carruthers came again to conduct her to his mistress. As the door to the duchess's room was opened, Harriet saw Lord Richard standing by the chimneypiece, leaning towards a woman well past the middle years, but whose expression was of great sweetness, which gave her countenance a look of charm and indeed beauty. The woman was fashionably dressed, but not in any *outré* way. As the door opened, the duchess looked across to Harriet and smiled. At once Harriet dropped a curtsy.

'Mamma, this is Miss Devenish,' Lord Richard said, coming forward and taking Harriet by the hand to lead her to his mother. 'Miss Devenish, this is my mother, the Dowager Duchess of Wartonshire.'

'How do you do, my dear?' Smiling, the duchess held out her hand and Harriet took it for a moment. Then the duchess turned towards her son. 'Miss Devenish has just left school, Richard?'

'Yes, Mamma.'

'And you, I collect, Miss Devenish, have-er-been writing letters to my son?'

'Yes, Your Grace.' Harriet blushed a little, and hurried on. 'At least, I did not know that there was any such person, but it became so disagreeable never to receive any letters, that at last I sent one to myself, and then, of course,

36

I had to reply. I-I took the name from a map of Cumberland we had in the schoolroom,' Harriet ended, a little breathlessly.

The duchess looked amused for a moment, then said seriously, 'I believe you wish to make enquiries as to your real guardian while you are in London, Miss Devenish?'

'Yes, Your Grace. I know of no kinsfolk in the world. Both my parents are dead, but somebody has arranged for money to be sent to Miss Bassenthwaite to pay for me, and the bank *must* know something of that!'

'It seems very likely. And it is certainly odd that they would tell Miss Bassenthwaite nothing, as she stood in place of a guardian to you. However, we will see what a little personal questioning may do. I quite see that you wish to know where you stand.'

'You are very kind, Your Grace,' Harriet said gratefully.

'Meanwhile, I would be delighted to have you with me—if you would care to stay,' the duchess continued. 'My children have all their own concerns to occupy them. It will be very pleasant for me to have a companion.'

Harriet looked from the duchess to her son and back again. Quite suddenly she felt very touched by the kindness of these strangers, and it was all she could do to blink back her quick tears.

The duchess smiled and leaned forward and patted Harriet's arm. 'I know that we shall get along famously, my dear. And we will go to Drummond's directly tomorrow morning.'

Three

The duchess was as good as her word. The next morning she summoned the carriage and accompanied Harriet to Drummond's Bank and asked to see Mr Andrew Drummond.

'It is a Mr Bacup, Your Grace, who has sent Miss Bassenthwaite the drafts. It used to be Mr Andrew Drummond, but he died some years ago,' Harriet whispered when they were alone in the waiting-room.

'He was perfectly in health last week, my dear. A great many of the Drummonds are called Andrew, and this particular one is the present senior partner. He is certain to know the full story,' the duchess whispered back.

The two ladies were ushered into a pleasant room looking out on Charing Cross, and were greeted by the senior partner. The duchess introduced Harriet, and after some pleasantries the duchess explained their business. Mr Bacup was summoned, and confirmed what Harriet already had said.

'To whose account are these drafts charged?' Mr Drummond asked the clerk.

But Mr Bacup was unable to tell anything further, his

responsibility beginning and ending with the sending of the draft.

Mr Drummond then summoned Mr Thurston, his senior clerk, who was equally ignorant, except that he was able to state that it was an arrangement that had been entered into by the late Mr Andrew Drummond.

Mr Thurston was dismissed, and Mr Drummond took out a large ledger from a locked drawer in his desk. He said apologetically, 'I must beg Your Grace to forgive me. It appears that the matter was some private arrangement entered into by my late kinsman.'

As he opened the ledger and looked into it, the duchess smiled at Harriet. Both ladies turned back to look at Mr Drummond as he gave a sort of grunt. His eyebrows had risen in what appeared to be great astonishment, and after a moment's looking, he closed the great book.

'I must apologize again, Your Grace, but—I am afraid I am unable to lay my hand at once on the information you require. In an arrangement like this, of long standing, the details are doubtless recorded in an old ledger which is not in daily use. May I suggest that I instigate a search, and I will notify Your Grace as soon as any information is to hand?'

The duchess frowned for a moment, but there seemed to be nothing else to do but accept the proposal, and she smiled graciously and agreed. 'I shall look forward to hearing from you very soon, sir. You will understand Miss Devenish's natural anxiety to know if any provisions have been made for her future.'

'Of course. Of course. I quite understand, Your Grace.'

After a few more pleasantries, the two ladies were ushered out to the carriage by Mr Drummond himself.

As they drove away, the duchess was silent, but Harriet

burst out, 'Your Grace, I do not understand it at all! I am convinced Mr Drummond saw something to the point in that ledger!'

'I had that idea also, my dear Harriet,' the duchess answered slowly.

'Then—why did he not tell us?'

'If you think a little, my dear, you will see why. At least, I may guess that it is that the donor wishes to remain anonymous. I dare say this Mr Andrew Drummond may not know anything personally of the matter, and will have to consult with his client, your benefactor, before he may tell us anything.'

'But surely, if somebody has been paying for me all these years, why should not they wish to be thanked for it?'

'I dare say the matter is not quite as simple as that, my dear.'

They discussed the matter all the way back to the duchess's house, but of course were unable to come to any conclusion. Lord Richard was waiting for them in Mersea Square, and when told what had happened said comfortably that he expected that it would all be settled very quickly.

'Indeed, I hope so!' Harriet remarked, 'For I should not wish to impose upon Her Grace!'

'It is no imposition, my dear. I have told you, I am very glad to have your company.' She turned to her son. 'And what do you propose to do today, Richard? No doubt you will be attending Jacksons as usual, and then—the Park?'

'I had thought to spend the day here, Mamma. And later, perhaps, Miss Devenish may like to accompany me when I drive.'

Harriet did not see the duchess's eyebrows rise as she answered excitedly, 'Oh, I would like that of all things, my lord! I expect you have a very elegant phaeton and the most spanking cattle! Are you a member of the Four in Hand Club?'

'I have a very decent equipage, and my horses are generally considered quite passable.'

'Oh, Richard!' the Duchess protested, smiling. 'You know very well there are none better! Why, you told me last week that Bennington wished to purchase them from you! You could scarcely have a greater compliment.'

'Certainly they suit me.'

'Miss Devenish,' the duchess went on, turning to Harriet, 'I warn you, when you drive with my son later, hold very tightly to the straps, and make sure you look straight ahead—or better still keep your eyes closed. On no account look down, or you will be sure to find your head swimming.

'Mamma!' Lord Richard cried reproachfully. 'You should give Miss Devenish that warning if ever she drives out with Talaton! He has come close to being upset twice this month to my certain knowledge.'

But when Harriet found herself seated beside Lord Richard later that day, and bowling through the Park behind the finest pair of horses she had ever seen and with a tiny tiger perched behind them, she thought she could enjoy no higher bliss. The sensation of speed was delightful to her, and her cheeks grew pink with excitement.

Lord Richard glanced at her, laughing. 'Well, Miss Devenish? You enjoy it?'

'Oh, my lord, it is intoxicating! Driving with Joshua was never like this!'

'I make no doubt of it!' Lord Richard laughed, pleased to see Harriet so happy, and also not unaware that the figure beside him was something of a cynosure. To see her seated beside Lord Richard would have been sufficient to attract interest in any case, though Harriet was not to know this. As a new and very pretty face, that interest must be compounded.

After completing one circuit, Lord Richard stopped to greet friends and gravely each time he presented Harriet as 'Miss Devenish, my ward.' Harriet smiled and sparkled and enchanted everyone.

'If Mamma agrees to bring you out,' Lord Richard said after one such meeting, 'I can see that you will be the rage of the season.'

'Oh! Do you really think Her Grace would agree? I should so love that!'

'I will have to speak to her about it.'

'How do you mean, I shall be the rage?'

'That, Miss Devenish, was the Marquis of Davenham. If he asks you to stand up with him, and I think he will, your success will be assured.'

Harriet frowned, puzzled. 'How can he do that, my lord?'

'Just by noticing you.'

'Is he so very fashionable, then?'

'A tip-top tulip, I promise you.'

'He looks rather old!'

'My own age, child!' Lord Richard returned, a trifle mortified.

'Oh, I beg your pardon! I did not mean . . . '

'You think me old, do you?'

'Not so *very* old. And I think you are quite the handsomest man I have ever met!'

Lord Richard stared at Harriet for a second, then burst out laughing as he looked ahead again.

'And are you—a tip-top tulip, my lord?'

Lord Richard shrugged, still laughing, but before he had time to answer, a young man on a magnificent chestnut slithered to a stop beside them, making Lord Richard pull up his own horses sharply.

'Good-day, Uncle!' the young man announced, doffing his hat and smiling at Harriet with very appreciative eyes.

'What do you mean, jumping on us like that, you young rapscallion!' Lord Richard returned somewhat wrathfully. 'You might have upset us!'

'Not you, Uncle!' the young man returned easily. 'You would never do anything so unhandy. Well? Are not you going to present me?'

Lord Richard glared for a moment, then said, 'Miss Devenish, this graceless fellow is my nephew, Talaton. This, George, is my ward, Miss Devenish.'

'Charmed, ma'am,' Lord Talaton bowed, his brown eyes speaking their admiration.

Harriet smiled and dimpled and thought the nephew even handsomer than the uncle. The same tall figure, the same dark hair, the same distinguished features. But—there was something in the look that was not the same, and which greatly appealed to Harriet.

'Your ward, Uncle!' Lord Talaton went on, clearly much astonished. 'Pray tell me, where have you been hiding Miss Devenish?'

'I have been living near Carlisle, my lord,' Harriet answered for herself.

'No wonder we have heard nothing of you then, ma'am. For shame, Uncle, hiding Miss Devenish away like that!'

'I have not been hiding Miss Devenish away as you call it, George! Miss Devenish has been at school in Cumberland, and has but just left it.'

'Well, I am delighted to make your acquaintance, Miss

43

Devenish. I am glad you have persuaded my uncle to bring you to London at last. You will be bringing Miss Devenish to my Mamma's thrash tomorrow, I suppose, Uncle? May I have the honour, Miss Devenish, of leading you out for the first dance?'

Harriet smiled blissfully, then looked doubtfully at Lord Richard.

'No, you may not!' Lord Richard said sharply. '*I* am leading out Miss Devenish for the first dance! If you behave, I may permit you to lead her out later.'

'Are you indeed!' Lord Talaton's eyebrows shot up to his hairline. 'I wonder what a certain party will have to say to that?'

Lord Richard looked as though he would make some very wrathful reply, but before he could utter a word, his nephew said to Harriet, 'Miss Devenish, ma'am, cut out as I am by my uncle, may I solicit for the second pair of dances at my Mamma's ball tomorrow?'

'You are very kind, my lord!'

Lord Richard glared at his nephew, and said sourly, 'The arrangement is conditional, George.'

'Upon what, Uncle?'

'Upon your behaviour, sir! And now, Miss Devenish and I wish to proceed, George. Good-day.'

'Of course, Uncle. Miss Devenish, your servant, ma'am.' And Lord Talaton doffed his hat again and bowed, his eyes merry as he looked at Harriet, as if they were sharing a secret joke. 'Good-day, Uncle.'

He drew his horse back a pace or two, and Lord Richard flicked his own horses to a trot. 'Insolent young puppy!' he fumed.

'I thought your nephew was very agreeable!' Harriet objected. 'I mean, it was very kind of him to offer to lead me out for the first dance. I am well aware how important the first dance is.'

'Well, *I* am going to lead you out!'

'So I collect. And I thank you very much for it. But—I would not wish you to quarrel with your friend because of it. I collect that Lord Talaton was implying that some other lady might expect you to lead her out?'

'Lord Talaton should mind his own business!' Lord Richard ground out furiously.

Harriet saw that Lord Richard was indeed quite enraged, and said to turn the subject, 'I did not know that I was to go to-to your sister's ball, my lord. I have not met her, of course.'

Lord Richard managed to speak naturally. 'Talaton's mother is my eldest sister, Mary. She is married to the Marquis of Ottery.'

'You have other sisters then, my lord?'

'Oh, indeed, yes. After Mary comes Elizabeth. My brother, Wartonshire, comes next, then Isabella, then Jane. Lastly, myself.'

'Are are all your sisters and brothers married?'

'Oh, yes, and all with families. I am the *youngest*,' he added meaningly, as an apparent afterthought. 'Talaton is less than ten years younger than I am.'

'Indeed!' Harriet would have liked to ask a great many questions about the viscount, but Lord Richard looked so vexed that she refrained. After all, she could always ask the duchess later.

The following morning Harriet and the duchess had scarcely finished breakfast when Lord Talaton was announced.

'This is an unexpected surprise, George!' the duchess

exclaimed. 'I had no idea that you were ever up and about so early!'

'Oh, pray do not rib me, ma'am. I always tell you that I am a deal more energetic than you give me credit for.'

'You already know Miss Devenish, I collect?'

'Yes, ma'am; my uncle introduced us yesterday—in the Park.' And Lord Talaton smiled at Harriet with a most speaking look. Harriet thought again what a very handsome man the viscount was.

'And to what do I owe this unexpectedly early call, George?'

'I have brought my mamma's card for this evening for Miss Devenish.'

'This evening?'

'The ball, ma'am! Oh, you had not forgotten! You do mean to come?'

'I—'

But the duchess got no further. 'I quite understood from my uncle yesterday that you were to bring Miss Devenish. After all, my uncle told me that I could not lead Miss Devenish out for the first dances, as he meant to do that himself, and that I must therefore be content with the second two. I am certain he believes that you are taking his ward.'

'I see,' the duchess said thoughtfully.

'I must say, Grandmamma, I do think it a huge joke to find that my uncle has had a ward tucked away in Cumberland for all these years, and that we have never heard anything of it. Mamma was totally astonished, and wondered why Wartonshire was not given the job.' And Lord Talaton looked brightly at Harriet, who went a little pink, and wondered if it would not have been a good deal easier not to continue the fiction that she was Lord Richard's ward. But

46

the duchess, who knew the truth, had thought it best to continue with the idea, as it would obviate much speculation as to why Harriet was in the dowager duchess's care.

'Well, it is none of your business, George,' the duchess said firmly.

'No, Grandmamma.' Lord Talaton smiled at Harriet. 'I was wondering, ma'am, if Miss Devenish would care to drive with me in the Park later today?'

'You will have to ask your uncle, George. He is Miss Devenish's guardian.' The duchess saw Harriet's disappointed look, and said, smiling, 'I do not think I would recommend it, my dear. George really is very likely to tip you out.'

'Oh, I say! That's coming it a bit strong, ma'am!' Lord Talaton cried indignantly.

'Her Grace advised me to hold on very tightly when I went out with—with my guardian yesterday,' Harriet twinkled.

'Yes, well, my uncle is a goer. But very steady.' Lord Talaton said with great fairness. 'I have never known him to have an upset.'

'Whereas the same can not be said of you,' the duchess remarked.

'That was not my fault, ma'am! That fool Belcher cut across me and I had no chance!'

'Well, I will certainly not give you permission to drive Miss Devenish. You must speak to your uncle first.'

A very great friend of the duchess's arrived then, and as the two older women were engaged in conversation, it was not long before Harriet and Lord Talaton drifted over to one of the windows for a tête-à-tête, while the other two had a comfortable doze on the sofa.

Harriet, never shy, chattered away to Lord Talaton as if

she had known him forever. He was so obviously admiring that the girl basked in his regard, innocently determined to add to her first favourable impression upon the viscount. She returned his banter lightly, and Lord Talaton thought that not only was his uncles's ward the prettiest girl of his acquaintance, but, an even greater recommendation, she was not one to sit mumchance like some females he knew, leaving all the effort of conversation to a fellow. In fact, the pair had an equally good opinion of each other, and there was a determination on both sides to further the acquaintanceship.

The two were still in deep conversation—deep, that is, only in the attention each paid the other, certainly not in subject matter—when Lord Richard arrived. They did not see him enter, and it was not until he was scarce a yard away and had uttered in very disapproving tones, 'Good morning, Miss Devenish,' that either of them became aware of him.

'Oh, good morning, my lord,' Harriet smiled, holding out her hand unaffectedly.

Sourly Lord Richard noticed that her cheeks were flushed and that her eyes were sparkling with pleasure. 'Good morning, Talaton,' he added shortly.

'Good morning, Uncle. How delightful to see you again! What a fine, bright day it is!'

Lord Richard looked at him suspiciously, then grunted.

'I came with a card for Mamma's ball for Miss Devenish, Uncle.'

'Did you indeed!'

'Yes, Mamma is vastly looking forward to meeting your ward. She is most anxious to know Miss Devenish.'

'I am not at all sure that Miss Devenish will be able to go.'

'Oh, Uncle! Why not?'

Harriet's own face fell. 'My lord?' she wavered.

'Because it may not have crossed your addle-pated skull that Miss Devenish had but just arrived in London, and has not yet had time to purchase any clothes.'

'But I have a ball-gown, my lord!' Harriet cried.

Lord Richard said somewhat stiffly, 'Forgive me, Miss Devenish, but—you have only just left school. And—I do not suppose that a gown purchased in Carlisle for a school-girl would be one that you would care to wear for a London ball.'

'I think Miss Devenish looks delightfully, Uncle!'

'So do I,' Lord Richard said, a little defensively.

'And it is a very pretty gown, my lord! I have worn it only once!'

'You mentioned nothing of this yesterdsay, Uncle! Why, you asked Miss Devenish to stand up with you for the first dances! Surely you would not be ashamed were your partner not in the very latest fashion! If that is the case, *I* would be only too pleased to lead Miss Devenish out at the first!' Lord Talaton said provokingly. He turned to Harriet. 'My uncle is famous for always being seen with creatures of the very highest elegance,' he went on. 'For my part, I care more about the inner quality of my partners. A pleasing appearance is but a fleeting, transient property,' Lord Talaton added with mock sanctimoniousness, and shooting a wicked smile at Harriet. 'Shame on you, Uncle . . . '

'Silence, sir!' Lord Richard rapped out furiously. 'This young cub is being deliberately provoking, ma'am. My thoughts were entirely for your own comfort, Miss Devenish. I know how much important ladies attach to being in the latest trim.'

'I would much rather go to the ball in my Carlisle gown, my lord, than not go at all!' Harriet assured Lord Richard.

'Of course you would!' Lord Talaton cried. 'Come, Uncle! Do not be such a curmudgeon!'

Lord Richard continued doubtful, but at length agreed sourly that Harriet should go to the ball.

'That is excellent!' the viscount exclaimed. 'Mamma's ball would have been a very tame affair if you had not come, Miss Devenish. Oh, one other thing, Uncle. I propose to take Miss Devenish driving in the Park later. I collect that you have no objection?'

Lord Richard's ire sprang to life again. 'Yes, I have, you young reprobate! I would not dream of permitting Miss Devenish to drive with you! It is my responsibility to keep her head safely on her shoulders, and if she drove out with you, I should not have one moment's ease.'

Harriet was deeply disappointed, but did not feel she could urge the proceeding herself, and nothing Lord Talaton could say would persuade Lord Richard to change his mind. It was exactly as if he were indeed her guardian, Harriet thought crossly, and had it not been for the duchess, Harriet might quite well have told Lord Talaton the truth. But her recollection of all that she owed that lady kept her silent.

She was exceedingly provoked when it turned out that Lord Richard was not intending to drive her himself; he had a prior engagement, he claimed, and Harriet had no option but to sit at home, thinking gloomily of what she was missing.

She felt slightly more in charity with her so-called guardian, however, when the duchess offered to lend Harriet a pearl necklace to wear at the ball, and it turned out that

Lord Richard had spoken to the duchess on the subject of Harriet's gown. She could not blind herself to his kind thought, and when she set out for the ball she felt herself to be the luckiest girl in the world. Here she was, going to her very first real ball; the duchess had pronounced her gown very charming and suitable for a first ball, and best of all, she knew that she was going to stand up with Lord Talaton.

Harriet thought herself in a fair way to falling in love with the young viscount.

He came up to her as soon as she and the duchess arrived in the ballroom, hovered about her while she was presented to his mother and father and his sisters, and remained with her while the duchess led the way to the seats for the chaperones. He stood then beside her chair, claiming her whole attention, so that she did not see Lord Richard bowing before her till he spoke.

'Have you no partner of your own to dance attendance on, George, but that you must monopolize mine?'

'You know that I have always admired your taste, Uncle, and have always tried to follow your lead in all things. How can you blame me now? Besides, Miss Devenish is quite the prettiest girl in the room.'

Harriet dimpled with pleasure. The music started then, and sets began to form.

Lord Richard bowed and held out his arm to Harriet. 'And Miss Devenish is *my* partner, George. *I* have the privilege of leading her out first.'

'You have an unfair advantage over me, Uncle,' Lord Talaton returned with a bold smile. 'But—my time will come.' And he gave Harriet a meaning grin.

Harriet laughed at him, then excused herself to the duchess, and very happily took Lord Richard's arm. She would soon be standing up with the young viscount, and meanwhile, Lord Richard was a very desirable partner. She could not help but be aware of all the heads turned to look at them.

'You are indeed in looks, Miss Devenish,' Lord Richard smiled.

'I thank you, my lord. I hope my—*gown*—does not cause you any distress?' she added naughtily.

'You little baggage!' Lord Richard laughed. 'You know very well it is quite charming, and I must congratulate the Carlisle dressmaker. It is the perfect gown for a first ball.'

'I am so glad you approve my lord. I should have been mortified indeed if you had felt ashamed of me!'

'Miss Devenish,' Lord Richard returned with a laugh tinged with wryness, 'I see you have picked up my reprobate nephew's manners very quickly. But, as your guardian, I warn you, I shall demand proper respect.'

Harriet smiled back. 'His lordship acknowledges that he follows your lordship in all things.'

Lord Richard laughed outright at that. 'Miss Devenish! I knew of your imagination. I had not before appreciated your powers of riposte!'

Harriet twinkled at her partner. Then over his shoulder she caught sight of Lord Talaton in conversation with a tall, very dark, very striking woman, dressed in a crimson silk gown with the highest possible waist, and with several vandyked flounces of black lace round the hem of the skirt. Satin slippers of the same crimson shade showed beneath the ankle-length skirt; a dazzling diamond tiara nestled in the dark hair, and a necklace of equally large diamonds caused the woman's neck to glitter as the stones caught the light from the hundreds of candles in the three huge chandeliers.

At once, Harriet wished she looked elegant and worldly like the woman in red. For a moment, her eyes were riveted by the creature, and abruptly the woman turned and stared directly at Harriet. The girl dropped her eyes in some confusion.

Lord Richard noticed this, followed her gaze, frowned, then caught her attention by remarking, 'I collect that you have had no message from Drummond's today?'

'No, my lord,' Harriet replied in a subdued voice.

Lord Richard kindly kept up the conversation, and in a moment Harriet was herself again, and able to ask her partner about his other sisters and his brother, the duke.

'Oh, Wartonshire will certainly not be here; he does not care for such affairs. In any case, his wife is sickly, and she does not go into society. She has produced five daughters, but no son, but I fear now she will never do that.'

'Then—that means, my lord—?'

'It is possible,' Lord Richard shrugged, and pointed out his sister, Lady Fitznorbert, who had just arrived.

The following dances with Lord Talaton were all that Harriet had hoped and expected. The young viscount kept her delightfully amused, and paid her a great deal of very obvious attention. He secured her for the supper dances, and when their own pair was ended, he presented his friends, and made sure that she was engaged for every dance, and covertly advised his friends that they were not to poach on his preserves.

As Harriet went into the supper-room on Lord Talaton's arm, she found as they edged their way forward that they were standing just behind the lady in the crimson gown. Harriet did not see at first who was her partner, but Lord Talaton cried in a hearty voice, 'Lady Charlotte, may I present to you my uncle's ward, Miss Devenish? Miss

Devenish, Lady Charlotte Logan. Lady Charlotte was so anxious to meet you.'

Harriet curtsied, and regarded the older woman with interest. She had never before met such a fashionable woman, and her earlier little confusion was quite gone.

'How do you do, my dear?' Lady Charlotte cooed, with a smile that did not reach her eyes. 'And so you are Richard Halton's ward! It came as the greatest possible astonishment to find that he had such a thing! He has kept it all an entirely close secret! And where is it he has been hiding you?'

As soon as Lady Charlotte looked at her, as soon as she heard the patronizing voice, Harriet knew that Lady Charlotte did not in the least like her. And nor did she like Lady Charlotte. But she answered quite equably, 'I have been at school in Cumberland, ma'am.'

'Not with Miss Bunbury, was it, my dear?'

Lord Talaton looked taken aback at that, and gave an embarrassed laugh, though Harriet could not understand why, and said seriously enough, 'No. It was with Miss Bassenthwaite's Academy I attended.'

'Ah, yes. Miss Bassenthwaite,' Lady Charlotte repeated. She turned and touched the arm of the gentleman behind her, whom Harriet now saw properly for the first time. 'Your ward is quite delightful, Richard,' Lady Charlotte purred with a smile. 'So pretty. And such a change to see you, my dear, with an *ingenue*.'

Lord Richard excused himself to the man he had been speaking with, and turned to join their group. His face was quite expressionless as he remarked, 'Oh, you have met Miss Devenish, Lady Charlotte? I quite agree with you. My ward is without doubt the most charming ornament to come to London society.'

Lady Charlotte gave an uncertain laugh, not looking best pleased.

Lord Talaton, however, saved her the need of replying by saying cheerfully, ''Pon my soul, Uncle, it is not often I hear you so poetic!'

'So it was you, was it, you young cub!' Lord Richard growled, looking far from pleased.

'What do you mean, dear Uncle? How have I offended you now?'

But Lord Richard did not answer him, but said to Lady Charlotte, 'Come, ma'am let us join our party.'

'Oh, but I would like to come to know your ward better, Richard. Do let us take supper together, the four of us. We can listen to Alvington boring us about his new cattle any day. I would much prefer to talk to Miss Devenish.'

It was plain to them all that Lord Richard would rather not have remained, but he could hardly depart in the face of Lady Charlotte's plainly expressed wish to stay. So the four sat down to supper together. Lord Richard was rather silent, but Lord Talaton made up for any deficiencies on his uncle's part, rattling away with hardly a pause, and Lady Charlotte plied Harriet with questions about the school and her relationship with Lord Richard to such a degree that Harriet, for all her usual composure, began to feel quite uncomfortable.

It was a relief to her when they were joined by Lord Richard's sister, Lady Isabella Fitznorbert and her husband, the Honourable John Fitznorbert. It was Lady Isabella's turn to monopolize Harriet in conversation then, asking quite as many questions as Lady Charlotte, but with so much obvious goodwill that Harriet did not mind in the least.

After supper, Harriet danced yet again with Lord Talaton, having quite overlooked the fact that three dances with one partner was not considered at all the thing. But Lord Richard did not come up to her again; indeed, he seemed to have disappeared from the ballroom entirely, and Harriet only discovered towards the end of the ball that he had retired to the cardroom.

But Harriet did not mind in the least. She found it absolutely delightful to flirt with Lord Talaton. By now, she had eyes for no—one else.

Four

Next morning the duchess and Harriet were seated in the morning-room after breakfast when the Duke of Wartonshire was said to be below.

'Pray ask His Grace to come up at once,' the duchess said to Carruthers, her voice expressing her surprise that her elder son had not come in at once.

'His Grace begs leave to speak with Your Grace in private,' Carruthers returned. 'His Grace is waiting in the library.'

'Indeed!' The duchess looked even more surprised. 'Oh, very well. Pray excuse me, Harriet, my dear.'

'Of course, Your Grace. But I can very well go elsewhere while His Grace comes to you here.'

'I would not dream of it, child. And when Wartonshire has finished, I shall bring him here to meet you.'

While the duchess was downstairs, Lord Talaton came, prepared to spend the rest of the morning gossiping about the ball.

'You were positively all the rage, Miss Devenish. I myself heard Davenham say that you were a damned fine-looking filly. Oh, pray excuse me, Miss Devenish, I merely repeat his lordship's words. He also said that he would certainly have stood up with you, had he been able to get *near* you! And my friend Benton was equally taken, Miss Devenish; but I warned *him* to keep his distance!'

'Oh, my lord!' Harriet laughed, much pleased.

'I did indeed! I am not having you swept away by one of my friends! I can hardly stop my uncle dancing with you as he is your guardian, but I mean to make certain you dance mainly with myself!' And Lord Talaton looked at her meaningly.

'Oh, my lord!' Harriet dimpled.

'Speaking of my revered uncle, where is he today? He has not come to see you yet?'

'No, my lord. You are the first caller. Or—nearly so.'

'Nearly so!' Lord Talaton began to look indignant.

'His Grace of Wartonshire has called upon Her Grace.'

'Oh, my other uncle! And what did you think of him?'

'I have not met him, my lord. He wished to speak to Her Grace in private.'

'Did he indeed! Well, he is not at all like my Uncle Richard, you know. In fact, he is a dashed dull dog—you have not missed anything. He takes after my late grandfather who was a pillar of rectitude in every way, and would as soon have died as wager so much as a farthing! He did not care for anything in the least lively. He had his head always in a book—and some dashed book of sermons, more often than not! He could have told you the names of the kings of Israel with all their children from Adam onwards, but scarce one time in five did he ever get my name right. And if ever I asked him which horse he fancied at Newmarket, he looked at me as if I were speaking of creatures from another planet!'

'And is his present Grace of Wartonshire interested in

scriptural genealogies also?' Harriet asked, thankful that she had picked on the duke's younger brother for guardian.

'No. Birds are his study. The feathered kind, of course. Dashed dull too. Do you know, Miss Devenish, he can see a dreary bundle of brown feathers at fifty yards and know if it is a thrush or a warbler or a sparrow? Never the least interest in any *lady*birds, though. Impeccably uxurious. I can not see the point of it, myself.'

'Lord Talaton!'

'Knowing about birds, I mean, Miss Devenish!'

'Oh, I see. And are-er-birds—all his grace's interest?'

'Indeed they are! And he is married to a creature who is quite as dull as his birds—my Aunt Amelia. She does not like to go out at all—will hardly appear in society—and my Uncle Wartonshire is content to stay with her. They suit each other very well.'

'He does not sound at all like his brother, Lord Richard!'

'Oh, he is not in the least. Different as chalk and cheese. My Uncle Richard would never remain faithful to one dull filly. Not that he would ever take up with a dull filly, mind. But—he is a proper tulip—my Uncle Richard!'

'I expect that he knows the Lady Charlotte Logan rather well?' Harriet ventured curiously.

'Oh, known her for years. She was married to Charles Logan—a great friend of my uncle's, but he was killed at Waterloo. In fact, I gather Charles Logan expired in my uncle's arms.'

'How very terrible! I suppose then he would be bound to lend a helping hand to his friend's widow.'

'Of course. My uncle is a good sort. But in Lady Charlotte's case, I think my uncle is only too happy to be of assistance.'

Harriet was not quite certain that she liked the way Lord

Talaton said this, and was glad that the duchess returned to the room just then. She affected surprise to see her grandson a second morning running, and said as much. Then she turned to Harriet. 'I am afraid Wartonshire had to hurry away, my dear, but I will have them both to dine here soon.

The duchess had scarcely returned when Lord Richard appeared. He gazed with a somewhat jaundiced eye at his young nephew. 'What! You here again, Talaton?' he grunted.

'Could you expect me to keep away, Uncle?' the young man rejoined with a wicked grin.

Lord Richard looked sourly, but the duchess broke in firmly, 'I must, however, ask you to go now, George. There is something which I must discuss privately with Miss Devenish.'

'Oh, I can wait till you are done, ma'am.'

'No, George. I do not know how long this will take.'

'Well, let me take Miss Devenish driving in the Park later, and I will go quietly.'

The duchess looked at Lord Richard, and that gentleman said very definitely, 'I would not dream of permitting it. You are far too harum-scarum with the ribbons, George.'

'Uncle!' Mock reproach filled the laughing eyes.

'Oh, be off with you!' cried the duchess. 'And if you promise to behave yourself, and not tease your uncle, you may dine here this evening.'

'Oh, ma'am!' Lord Talaton cried extravagantly; 'You have made me the happiest of men! Goodbye for the present, Lovely Miss Devenish! The hours will pass with leaden feet till I see you again. Goodbye, Uncle. Your words have wounded me to the quick.'

Lord Richard vouchsafed no reply, but merely grunted.

Harriet curtsied laughing to Lord Talaton, happy to know that she would see him later in the day.

When he was gone, Harriet turned enquiringly to the duchess, thinking that she must have news from Drummond's. But such turned out to be not the case, for the duchess began to question her about her parents.

'Are you sure you can remember nothing of your parents, my dear?'

'Nothing more than I have told you already, ma'am.'

'You have not heard your father's name?'

Harriet looked puzzled. 'You mean his Christian name, Your Grace?'

The duchess nodded and Harriet had to admit her ignorance.

'And your mother? You know nothing of your mother at all? Not her maiden name?'

Again Harriet shook her head. 'I was never told anything, ma'am; and I do not believe Miss Bassenthwaite knew anything either.'

'No recollections from your earliest days?'

Yet once more Harriet disclaimed knowledge. The duchess looked somewhat distrait, and then Lord Richard, to Harriet's relief, asked the duchess if she had had news from the bank.

'No . . . I have heard nothing from the bank.'

Harriet heard this curiously, and looked at Lord Richard. But he was regarding his mother, whose face was impassive. 'Is there any particular reason for these questions, ma'am?' he asked quietly.

But the duchess shook her head and excused herself. Harriet looked at Lord Richard considerably bewildered.

'I-I know that Her Grace said that she had heard nothing, my lord, but—don't you think—I mean—?'

'I do not know, Miss Devenish. But I think I had better find out.' And Lord Richard strode firmly from the room.

But the week continued with no further news from the bank, and Harriet remained puzzled. The duchess made no attempt to explain her questions, and Lord Richard did not refer to the matter again. So the girl put the matter from her mind as far as she could.

In this she was greatly helped by the attentions of Lord Talaton, which continued as they had begun. He was constantly at his grandmother's house, always suggesting amusements for her diversion. It was through him that Harriet went to the exhibition of wild animals in the Strand; she was startled and at first frightened when a lion let out a huge roar just behind her, and she was exceedingly glad of the protecting arm of the young viscount.

It was Lord Talaton who arranged for the duchess and Harriet to visit Vauxhall, which Harriet thought was the most beautiful garden she had ever seen, with all the thousands of lights, and the lively music. At every turn there was some fresh wonder: a gigantic waterfall; an orchestra perched high above them so that the sound appeared to come out of the trees; acrobats performing the most incredible, alarming feats, so that she was glad to cling to Lord Talaton for fear of fainting with fright and excitement.

It was the same young gentleman who procured seats at Astleys, where Harriet thrilled at the sight of the elegant horses carrying gauze-clad dancers round the amphitheatre on their bare backs, and other horses dancing to the music of the waltz and the gavotte.

All in all, Lord Talaton made a very great effort to entertain Harriet, and whatever he suggested she knew would be great fun, and very likely exciting as well.

She was taken out sometimes by Lord Richard also. He escorted her to the opening of the new season's exhibition at the Royal Academy, but Harriet could not enjoy it. It was filled with fashionable people, but was so crowded and stuffy that she saw scarcely one picture, and felt quite like fainting from the heat.

Lord Richard also took her to see Westminster Abbey and the tombs of the Kings of England, and to the lobby of the Houses of Parliament where she saw the Prime Minister, Lord Liverpool, already looking an old man after all the cares of the war years.

Harriet endeavoured to appear polite as Lord Richard showed her the sights of London, and she was duly impressed when he took her first to Pudding Lane, and then to the very top of the Monument to the Fire of London, from which she had a magnificent view of the City; and again when he escorted her to see the gas lighting in Pall Mall. But it was Lord Talaton who proposed the really exciting schemes, and whose company Harriet found infinitely more thrilling.

Since Lady Ottery's ball, the duchess had taken Harriet to no more evening functions. The duchess herself did not go out a great deal, and she confessed to Harriet that she was somewhat at a loss to know how to proceed.

'You see, you are not out, Harriet, my dear, and I am not certain that I should take it upon myself to launch you. It is not that I am at all unwilling to do so—but—your real guardian may come forward, and—well, you can see that that would make for a very difficult situation. The fiction that you are my son's ward will serve so long as you do not go into society—so long as you meet but few people. I confess I had hoped that after Lady Ottery's ball, we might have heard something; but—until we have definite news, I really do not feel I can take it upon myself to do anything.'

Harriet assured the duchess that she was very happy to continue as she was. 'After all, ma'am, I had not thought to come out.'

'That is true. But—now that you are with me, it will look very odd if you do not come out properly. Besides, you should be presented: you should go to balls: you are just the right age to enjoy them. I must say, I do feel that whoever is responsible for you is very amiss! It really is high time that something was done!' The duchess looked quite vexed. 'I agreed that you should go to my daughter's ball as the season had hardly started, and—well, it was a family affair—but—'

'But I never had the least expectation of being presented, Your Grace!' Harriet gasped, wishing very much that Susan Holt could hear this conversation.

'Not the thing at all!' the duchess murmured, tapping her finger with annoyance.

The duchess sent an urgent note to Drummond's, but the only reply it elicited was another bland note regretting that there was no news at the moment.

As the month went by, Harriet could not help wishing that the duchess did not feel so very nice about launching her into society. Now that the season was in full swing, she grew increasingly aware of what she was missing. She tried not to feel ungrateful, but with Lord Talaton dashing off to some ball every night, she was seeing him only during the day; and though he continued to spend every day with her, regaling her with descriptions of all the delights she was missing, she was unable to repress her increasing longing.

Lord Talaton was obviously popular, and Harriet could

not help but think of all the beautiful young women he must dance with, and she craved to be of that number herself. In spite of all her good resolutions, Harriet's yearning grew.

She was, therefore, immediately tempted when one evening Lord Talaton came to his grandmother's house with the proposal that she should accompany him to the masquerade at the Opera House. Harriet was alone when Lord Talaton arrived, the duchess having gone to visit Lady Ottery who was it appeared much worried about her youngest daughter.

'Oh, Lord Talaton! It sounds the very greatest fun!'

'It will be.'

'I have never been to a masquerade!' Harriet cried, her eyes shining. Then her shoulders slumped. 'I should so like to have gone!'

'My dear Miss Devenish, what is there to stop you?'

'You know that I have not come out yet, my lord!'

'I am certain that my grandmother would not object to this. After all, you would be disguised!'

'But—Her Grace is not here!'

'So?'

'I can not ask her. Her Grace is with Lady Ottery.'

'With Mamma! Then you may depend upon it that my grandmother will be there all evening. There never was such a one for going on as my Mamma. We had better leave at once if we are to go.'

'But—I could not go without Her Grace's permission!'

'Oh, come, Miss Devenish! I will be with you. You know Her Grace will not mind a scrap if I am there to look after you. Did not she herself come to Vauxhall when we went?'

'Yes, but—'

'I have a domino all ready for you, Miss Devenish,' Lord Talaton said coaxingly, 'It is in the chaise. Oh, do come, Miss Devenish!'

Harriet hesitated still.

'You came to my Mamma's ball!' Lord Talaton urged.

'That was different. A-a family party.'

'There were many who were not our kinsfolk there!'

'I did not suppose that you were connected with quite everyone in London!' Harriet laughed.

'With a goodly number, I assure you! But, do come, dearest Miss Devenish! After all, what harm can it do—when I shall be with you? And you will not be recognized, of course. Oh, do come, ma'am! I am convinced that Her Grace would not object!'

'Well—' Harriet said slowly, greatly tempted.

'Please, Miss Devenish!' Lord Talaton urged. 'It would be a wretched evening without you!' And Lord Talaton caught hold of Harriet's hands and gazed down into her face with his most speaking glance.

Harriet was lost. She was not proof against the viscount's cajoling. She could not have said no when Lord Talaton looked at her in that manner for all the gold in the Bank of England.

'Very well! I will come! But—I must not be back late. I must leave a note for Her Grace.'

'*I* will write one for you while you fetch your reticule and your shawl.'

Harriet sped upstairs, leaving Lord Talaton to pen the message, and when she came downstairs again, he was waiting for her in the hall. He took her hand and tucked it through his arm.

'Dearest Miss Devenish! We will have the most wonderful time!'

Happily, Harriet smiled back, and bade goodnight to Carruthers who was holding the door for them.

'We are going to a masquerade, Carruthers,' Harriet said gaily. 'At the Opera House. Is not that it, my lord?'

Before the servant had time to answer, Lord Talaton hurried Harriet out of the house and into the waiting chaise, and gave the order to start at once. 'There was no need to tell Carruthers where we are going!' Lord Talaton remarked, a trifle red.

'He has been very kind to me. He will be glad to know that I am going to enjoy myself,' Harriet smiled.

'But—' Lord Talaton looked less than pleased.

'I am sorry if you did not like it my lord; but—I do not see the harm.'

Lord Talaton clearly roused himself with an effort. He smiled brilliantly. 'No, of course it did not matter. Not in the least. Look; here is your domino. It is one my mamma used to wear, but I dare say it will fit.' Harriet pulled the garment over her head and settled the half—mask across her eyes. 'How do I look, my lord?'

'Delightfully—as ever, Miss Devenish,' Lord Talaton replied promptly, and seized her hand and carried it to his lips.

Harriet felt herself blushing as she saw the ardour in the young man's eyes, and suddenly embarrassed, she pulled her hand away. 'Will not you put on your own domino, my lord?'

The viscount did so, and enveloped in the black cape, Harriet hoped that she was as unrecognizable as was his lordship now. She felt a little tremor or two as to the rightness of what she was doing, but stifled them quickly, and thought only of the pleasure ahead. She smiled at Lord Talaton. He gave her an answering smile, his teeth gleaming whitely as he smiled, and his hidden eyes glittering behind their mask.

They arrived at the Opera House to find it bursting at the doors with the press. Spectators crowded the boxes, hanging over to watch the animated scene below, and the floor was as full as it was possible to be. A quadrille was in progress as they arrived, but it ended very soon; another band replaced the first, and the strains of a waltz rang out.

Lord Talaton bowed to Harriet. 'May I have the honour, Miss Devenish?'

Harriet smiled and curtsied and held out her arms, and Lord Talaton swung her onto the floor, and whirled her about the room till her head was spinning.

'I say, Miss Devenish, you must have waltzed very often before!'

'Only once or twice, my lord.' This was true. And only at impromptu dances when Harriet had visited the home of her friend, Blanche Sawston, and had waltzed with Blanche's brothers.

'I knew it must be so. You do not lean upon me as so many females do!'

It was exhilarating twirling about the room like this, and being in the centre of a throng of people disguised as she was, added to the excitement. Harriet's eyes were shining like diamonds when the dance was ended.

'You are glad you came, Miss Devenish? This is a great deal better, is not it, than sitting at home alone in Mersea Square?'

'Oh, indeed it is! I think waltzing is the most exciting thing in the world! It-it is almost like flying!'

Lord Talaton laughed at her enthusiasm, and suggested that she might like some refreshment. It was certainly very hot underneath the black dominoes, and Harriet was thankful to rest.

But as soon as the band struck up again, she was ready to dance once more.

This time it was a country dance, one in which the outer circle of ladies moved round to their right, so that by the end of the dance, Harriet was several couples away from Lord Talaton. She looked for him anxiously, but the man opposite whom she had finished the dance, took her by the arm and bending down so that his face was close to hers said, 'Let us take a little walk together, my pretty. I make no doubt but that you would feel refreshed after some wine?'

'Oh, no! I thank you, sir, but I must get back to my companion.' And Harriet tried to free herself from the man's grasp.

'There is no need for any hurry, my dear,' the wretched man went on, leering at her. 'I can not see any young blade hurrying to you. Come with me, and let us have a comfortable little talk together while we drink some wine.'

And the odious man gripped Harriet's arm more firmly, and propelled her from the floor.

'Oh, no, sir! Please, I pray you, let me go! My companion will be with me in a moment!'

And Harriet struggled to free herself. But the man proceeded regardless, and none of those they passed took any notice of Harriet's squirming. All around her were laughing mouths and loud voices, and suddenly Harriet thought the dominoes looked sinister, where before they had looked only excitingly mysterious.

'Let me go, sir!' she cried loudly now, almost hysterical with fright. 'Let me go!'

But the man who had her in his grip was big and strong

and only laughed as she twisted to get away. He dragged her across the floor towards a door to the boxes, pulled her through it, then hauled her up the stairs to the first tier. There he opened the door to one of the boxes, thrust her inside, then closed the door upon the two of them.

Harriet felt a slight touch of relief to see that there were already four other persons in the box; two men and two women, seated on chairs and with wineglasses in their hands.

'Well, Ned, and who is this?' one of the men laughed, eyeing Harriet boldly, and not rising, but keeping his arms about the waist of one of the females.

'Now, then, my pretty, what's your name?' demanded the man who had dragged her to the box.

Harriet's heart was still beating wildly, and she continued to feel very afraid. The two other women, she had seen at a glance, and in spite of the masks they wore, had flushed faces, and from their attitudes, she thought they must be foxed. The third man there, who looked more gentlemanly in appearance at least, raised his glass and inspected Harriet insolently.

The man holding her shook her arm roughly. 'Speak up, my beauty.

'I had thought this a masquerade, sir,' Harriet answered as boldly as she could.

'But I have a mind to see you now,' the man grunted, making as though to pull aside her mask.

'Gently, Ned, gently,' the man with the glass remonstrated. 'The young lady is quite right; it is not time to unmask yet. Sit down, my dear,' he went on, turning to Harriet with a smile, which made Harriet shiver more than the previous roughness of the man called Ned. 'Allow me to pour you some wine.'

And he picked up a glass and poured out a quantity of golden liquid and held the drink out to Harriet.

'Thank you, sir, but I am not thirsty.'

The man's eyes flickered behind the mask. 'Do not you find it warm in here, ma'am?'

'Indeed, yes, sir.'

'Then you'll have the drink that my friend offers you!' And the man holding onto Harriet sat down and pulled her onto his knee. Then he took the glass from the other man and thrust it against Harriet's lips. Harriet turned her head away, and the contents of the glass spilled down her domino.

The others laughed. Harriet struggled to free herself, her heart thumping more wildly than ever. She had never encountered such people as these in her life, and she knew not what to do. Instinctively now she shouted at the top of her voice. 'Help me! Will not someone help me?' And she attempted to rise, but the man pulled her back with a coarse laugh.

Gathering her scattered wits together, Harriet cried as bravely as she could manage, 'If you do not let me go, you will be sorry for it, sir!'

'Oh, shall I, indeed!' the man roared with a belly laugh. 'Come, my beauty, that's more what I like to see. There's nothing like a young gentry mort when she flies up into the boughs. The sport is all the better then.' And the wretched man pulled Harriet close to him and attempted to kiss her.

Harriet turned her head away quickly, disgusted by the coarse face and the rum-smelling breath. As the man's wet lips landed on the shoulder of her domino, she punched him as hard as she could in the stomach.

The man let out a shriek of pain and clasped his belly with both hands. In a flash Harriet was up and reaching for the door handle, but now the man who had given her the wine seized her arm.

'Let me go, sir! Oh, pray, let me go! As you are a gentleman, sir!'

'Tell me what a young thing like you is doing at a rout like this,' the man drawled, not releasing Harriet's arm.

'I came—with a friend, sir,' Harriet gasped. 'Oh! You hurt my arm, sir! And if you do not let me go, I will serve you the same as your friend!'

'Oh, I think not, my dear.' Easily, contemptuously, he seized Harriet's other hand, and held the two as in a vice. For all his gentlemanly clothes, the man's fingers felt strong as steel.

Frantically now Harriet sought to free herself, but the man held her without difficulty. Disdainfully, he turned to the other four, the man whom Harriet had struck still rubbing and groaning. 'I'll leave you two with these rum doxies. I think this little rainbow more to my taste. I had not expected such luck here tonight.'

And with that he flung open the door and pulled Harriet out of the box.

Now that she was alone with this man, Harriet was more frightened than ever. But there were other people in the corridor, and Harriet screamed out to them to help her.

Several of the people turned to watch, laughing, and making no movement to aid her.

'Oh, will not one of you help me?' Harriet appealed.

But still nobody moved, and her captor drew her effortlessly along the corridor.

'If you are not silent at once, I will silence your tongue for you!' Harriet's captor suddenly hissed. 'I can not abide a screaming female.'

Harriet saw his angry eyes behind the mask, and fell

abruptly silent, terrified that the man would carry out his threat in some unspeakable way. She tripped along the passage beside the man till they came to the door of another box, which the man proceeded to open, and drew her inside. Still holding her he pushed the door closed, and Harriet heard a click as though a bolt were being shot home.

She screamed out again now, her fear of the man's intentions being greater than her fear of his violence.

'Be silent, my girl! I have warned you that it will be the worse for you!' And the man spun Harriet round and clasped one hand across her mouth and pushed her down onto one of the chairs in the box, which seemed much larger and more elaborately furnished than the previous one.

Harriet attempted to struggle, but her hands were held fast, and the whole weight of the man held her still.

Suddenly she heard running feet in the passage outside the box, and a well-known voice shouted 'Harriet' Where are you?'

At the shout, for a moment the man's hand across her mouth slackened a little, and instinctively, more than by intention, Harriet managed to close her teeth on one of the man's fingers.

He pulled his hand away quickly. 'You little devil!' he hissed.

But Harriet took no notice. She shouted loudly, 'I am here, my lord! Oh! Come quickly!'

The next moment the man had fastened his hand over her mouth again, cruelly forcing her jaws together, the fingers digging into her flesh, and stilling her flailing feet by catching them between his legs.

The running feet came to a halt outside the door. 'This one I think, George!' the same voice said. Then loudly

73

again, 'Harriet? Are you in there?' And the handle of the door rattled.

Harriet tried to move and cry out, but her voice was only a gurgle in her throat. The man holding her remained motionless, eyes glittering fiercely through his mask.

There came the sound of the heavy bodies hurling themselves against the door. To Harriet's joy there came a splintering of wood and Lord Richard followed by Lord Talaton burst into the room.

At the sight of the two intruders, the man holding Harriet made as if to put his hand into a pocket. But before his hand was more than halfway to its goal, Lord Richard struck the man a powerful blow on the jaw. The man attempted to ward him off, and aimed a blow at his opponent.

But the man was no match for the enraged lord. Another blow landed on the man's head, and he stumbled backwards till stopped by the wall of the box. Lord Richard strode after him, yanking him up by his domino, and delivered a third blow at which the man sank slowly down the wall to the floor, senseless.

'Well done, Uncle!' Lord Talaton's voice came excitedly. 'Oh! that was a famous hook! Jackson himself could not have done better!'

Lord Richard bent down and slipped the mask from the man's face before he turned to face his nephew. Harriet herself was now enfolded in the viscount's arms, panting heavily, tears of relief running down her face, little sobs issuing from her throat.

Lord Richard's countenance took on an even grimmer look now. 'Be silent, sir! You have done damage enough for this evening. Did this fellow—harm you, Miss Devenish?'

Harriet shook her head and mumbled through her sobs. 'No, my lord. But I do not know what he might have done had you not arrived in time!'

'Very likely,' Lord Richard said grimly. He shot a glance at Harriet, then continued in the same voice, 'Well, you had better follow me.' And with that, he opened a second door at the back of the box, which led onto a corridor with a staircase a short distance ahead. Lord Richard marched through this door without glancing at the other pair again. They followed, subdued now, but for Harriet's sniffs.

At the bottom of the staircase Lord Richard, hardly glancing at them, ordered, 'Wait here!' And disappeared through another door.

When they were alone, Harriet looked up at Lord Talaton and whispered, 'Oh, I wish I had never come!'

'There is no need for you to fear my uncle,' Lord Talaton whispered back. 'He will never be angry with you. It is I who will have to bear all his wrath.'

'I-I was not thinking of Lord Richard.'

'Oh, to be sure, you must have had a very unpleasant experience. But—why did you go off with the fellow like that?'

'I did not "go off" with him!' Harriet cried indignantly, snatching her arm away from Lord Talaton's supporting one. 'He made me! And I could not see you anywhere, my lord!'

'I looked about everywhere for you, but you were nowhere to be seen! And when my uncle stood suddenly before me, and demanded to know where you were, and I had to say that I did not know, well, I have never seen him in a greater passion.'

'Well, I am thankful that he did arrive, or I shudder to think what might have happened to me!'

'Oh, *I* should have found you soon enough, Miss Devenish,' Lord Talaton said comfortably. 'But, why you went off with that fellow, I can not think.'

'I did not go off with him!' Harriet returned again indignantly. And was about to say a good deal more, when the door opened again and Lord Richard stood there.

'The carriage is outside,' he said curtly. 'Get into it at once.'

Unable to meet his eyes, Harriet hurried past him with head averted and did as she was bid. She was followed by Lord Talaton who seemed very sheepish.

'Sit over there, Talaton,' Lord Richard ordered, then followed them in, his face grim, and seated himself beside Harriet. The door was closed upon them, and almost at once the carriage moved off.

'Take off those things,' Lord Richard ordered, removing his own domino. 'I suppose it was your shatter-brained idea that you should take Miss Devenish to the masquerade?' he went on, glaring at his nephew.

'I thought Miss Devenish would enjoy it!' Lord Talaton answered in an attempt to justify himself. 'She has a dull time of it with the duchess. She never goes to any balls—!'

'There is reason enough for that!' Lord Richard retorted sharply. 'And you, Miss Devenish,' Lord Richard went on, turning to Harriet, 'is this the way you repay my mother's kindness to you, sneaking off like that?'

'Her Grace was not at home! I could not ask her!' Harriet answered, feeling injured as well as ashamed.

'And do you think that she would have given you permission, knowing that she did not feel that she could bring you out? You must know that she has turned down other invitations for you—respectable invitations—'

Suddenly Harriet was only ashamed. 'Respectable?' she asked faintly.

'Yes, respectable!' Lord Richard said angrily. 'Surely you must know that well-bred young ladies do not go to routs accompanied only by a ramshackle fellow such as Talaton here?'

'Oh, I say!' Lord Talaton began to protest.

'Be silent, sir!' thundered Lord Richard now. He turned back to Harriet. 'Even at Miss Bassenthwaite's, I should have thought you would have learnt a simple thing like that! Had you had the least scintilla of sense—let alone sensibility—you would never have gone! I am surprised at you, Miss Devenish! Though why I should be,' he went on after a moment, 'I am at a loss to understand. From the moment I met you, you seemed bent on getting your own way. This—escapade—is quite of a piece with your previous conduct.'

Harriet, overwrought by all that had happened to her, and now suffering Lord Richard's anger and the lash of his tongue, now burst into noisy tears.

'Now look what you have done, Uncle!' Lord Talaton protested.

'Be silent, sir!' Lord Richard roared. 'Be silent, and I will tell you both what you will do, so that the affair may bring as little upset as possible upon the person I would most wish to shield. Now, Miss Devenish, am I correct in thinking that you did not at any time unmask?'

Harriet was beyond speech, managed only to shake her head and sniff loudly.

'Very well. Now, listen to me, both of you. We shall say nothing of this affair—to *anyone*. Is that understood? It will be expunged—as though it had never happened. I have no wish to have the duchess upset by her learning of what has occurred. Now, do you both promise?'

Harriet, who had been dreading having the duchess know of the escapade, felt this was more than she could have dared hope for, and nodded quite vigorously.

'Talaton? Have I your promise?'

Lord Talaton, upon whom it had now been borne sufficiently, that the masquerade was not an entertainment suitable for a young lady, assured his uncle that he had indeed that promise, albeit a little sulkily.

'I do not know if Her Grace will be returned when we reach Mersea Square, but whether she is or no, Miss Devenish, you will go to bed immediately. *I* will make whatever explanations are necessary to my mother. As for you, Talaton, I shall call upon you at eleven o'clock tomorrow morning precisely. I expect you to be in and ready to receive me. If you are not up, I promise you I shall haul you out of bed in order to tell you what a ramshackle business this has been. How you could think to involve Miss Devenish in such a havey-cavey affair I am at a loss to understand. I had hoped—though I had not much confidence—that you had more sense.'

Lord Richard continued in this manner till the carriage stopped to leave Lord Talaton at his home, then went the short distance to the duchess's house. Harriet sat silently, feeling very wretched and a little sorry for herself. Lord Richard had been very harsh, she thought, for what had been meant only as an evening's fun.

Lord Richard sat silent also. Harriet was very conscious of his grim figure near her, and after some moments ventured to peep at him. She was dismayed to see that he looked as stern as ever.

'I-I have not thanked you yet for rescuing me, my lord,'

she murmured timidly at last, anxious to break the overbearing silence.

Lord Richard glanced at her briefly, then looked away again, his face unsmiling. 'It is well I arrived when I did, I think,' he replied brusquely. 'Rakewell is a notorious libertine.'

Harriet was too oppressed to say anything more at once. But after a while she asked timidly, 'How-how did you know where to find us, my lord?'

'Luckily you had mentioned to Carruthers where you were going. I confess at first I thought the old fellow had made a mistake.'

'I wonder if perhaps you had seen the note Lord Talaton left for the duchess.'

'He left a note!'

'Yes, my lord.'

'Then I pray that my mother may not be returned!'

In Mersea Square they found that this was the case, and Harriet was thankful to scuttle off to bed, out of Lord Richard's disapproving presence. But it was a long time before she fell asleep. The terror she had felt when she had thought she was going to be ravished had faded a little, and her greatest discomfort was due to her knowledge that she had lost Lord Richard's good opinion of her. She was surprised to find how much this knowledge hurt.

Five

Harriet had not the least wish to meet Lord Richard the following morning, but even less did she wish to meet the duchess. However, she could not avoid seeing the latter, and, with a good deal of trepidation went to the duchess's room as usual. But there was positively no alteration in the duchess's manner towards her: the older woman's face was as kindly and smiling as ever, and Harriet breathed a sigh of relief that Lord Richard had decided to act as he had. Far worse than the actual events now to Harriet was the consciousness of her own discourtesy to the duchess.

And the girl felt that coals of fire were being heaped upon her head for, in reply to Harriet's inquiry as to how Lady Ottery's daughter did, the duchess replied, 'I am sorry that I was away so long, my dear. You must have had a very dull time of it. But, when I am with my daughter, I am afraid we chatter away like two old washerwomen.'

Harriet could not help blushing, and kept her head down till the hot tide had receded. It was plain, now, that Lord Richard had not spoken to his mother the previous evening.

After breakfast Harriet sat in the morning-room with her work-basket. This was not an occupation she enjoyed at all, but guilt made her dutiful, and she worked diligently on items for the duchess's poor basket, dull work, hemming shifts and seaming petticoats.

The duchess was busy in her own room with her correspondence, and Harriet had plenty of time to reflect upon her escapade. Sometimes she hoped that Lord Richard would call that morning, so that they might become friends and be comfortable together again. But more often she dreaded such an encounter; it would be terrible to have to endure a repetition of Lord Richard's angry words of the previous evening, and she felt that she would never be able to look Lord Richard in the eye again.

At eleven o'clock she imagined Lord Richard calling upon his nephew, and felt distinctly sorry for the young man. Perhaps Lord Talaton would come to Mersea Square later himself. Harriet coloured deeply as she recollected how she had flung herself into the viscount's arms the previous evening while his uncle was dealing with her would-be seducer.

But she could not help smiling also at the recollection. It had been an exceedingly pleasant experience—almost pleasant enough to make up for the terror which had occasioned the circumstance of her being in Lord Talaton's arms.

Harriet was re-living the experience and smiling quietly to herself, her hemming lying forgotten in her lap, when Lord Richard was announced.

In a flurry, Harriet jumped to her feet, clutching the sewing to her, and managed some sort of curtsy. She gazed hesitantly at his lordship, uncertain whether he meant to scold her or not, and could not quite meet his eyes.

'Well, Miss Devenish?' Lord Richard enquired, not at

all in a scolding sort of voice, but—almost sadly, Harriet noticed, surprised.

She looked into his face quickly. 'Well, my lord?' She endeavoured to smile.

'I trust you are feeling better this morning?'

'Yes, I thank you, my lord.'

Lord Richard turned away then, and went to stand by the window, staring out, his hands clasped behind his back. Harriet watched him somewhat fearfully, wondering if he was gathering himself together preparatory to launching a scold.

But when he had remained so for several minutes without saying a word, Harriet ventured to sit down again, and busied herself attempting to re-thread her needle which had become unthreaded when she had jumped up.

She found the normally simple task very difficult because her eyes were now blinded by tears. She brushed them away with the back of her hand and took a deep breath to steady herself. She glanced across to the window and saw that Lord Richard was watching her.

'Will-will not you be seated, my lord?' she asked in a forced bright voice.

The man did not reply, but regarded her for some moments, then slowly crossed the floor and seated himself in a chair opposite her. He folded his arms and continued to regard her. Harriet could not meet his gaze boldly, but her look darted to his face, and she felt sadly discomfited by the silent figure. She busied herself once more trying to get the recalcitrant thread through the eye of the needle.

'Miss Devenish,' Lord Richard said at last, 'I-I may have spoken harshly last night—more harshly than I had any right to do. After all, I have no legal right to claim your obedience—we both know that my calling myself your guardian started as a joke. Perhaps it is time it was brought to an end.'

Harriet felt hollow inside. 'Oh, my lord! I would be—that is—after all your kindness, my lord, I would *wish* to do as you would like. Last night—I did not think. I-I was tempted when Lord Talaton suggested that we should go to the masquerade. I had been sitting by myself, feeling very dull, when his lordship came and . . . ' Harriet's voice faded away.

'I think that my mother and myself have not considered sufficiently how dreary it must be for you to live with a woman old enough to be your grandmother—'

'Oh, no, my lord!' Harriet burst out. 'Her Grace has been everything that is kind! I would not like you to think—I mean, I have been very happy here. And I have done so many things. We go shopping and calling, and with Lord Talaton we have been to Astleys, and to the Exchange and Vauxhall, and you have taken me to the Houses of Parliament and the Abbey and Whitehall—I have had a very great deal of entertainment.'

'The Abbey and Whitehall and the seat of government must have seemed dry indeed compared with Vauxhall and Astleys and wild animals!' Lord Richard said wryly.

'Oh, no, my lord! I was most interested!' Harriet cried, anxious that she should not seem ungrateful. 'You have all been so kind. I am always conscious of the fact that I am a stranger, and that you are under no obligation to do anything for me at all!'

'Do you really think of me—of us—as strangers, Miss Devenish?' Lord Richard asked with a quick, melancholy look.

'Oh, no, my lord! Not now! Of course not! What I mean

is—we were strangers, and I had no claim on you—for anything!'

'Well, well,' Lord Richard said, rising, and going to look out of the window again. 'I shall speak to my mother. And I shall go and see Drummond myself. This has been going on long enough now, and I shall force him to speak— if I have to choke it out of him.'

'I do indeed think it odd, my lord. And—if there is no more money for me, the sooner I find myself some kind of situation, the better it will be.'

'But—what could you do?' Lord Richard smiled indulgently.

'Oh, I know I am not trained for anything really—but— I could perhaps be a companion.'

Lord Richard smiled broadly. 'Well, there is no need for us to think of anything of the kind yet. I shall go directly to Drummond and ask him what he is about. Really, I can not understand the man. I have never known him so dilatory before. And meanwhile, Miss Devenish, you may continue as companion to my mother, who, I know, is very glad to have you here.' And Lord Richard came forward and took Harriet's hand.

'You are going so soon, my lord? You will not see Her Grace?'

'I will certainly see her before I go, Miss Devenish. And pray, do not look so melancholy. Last night's escapade is now entirely forgotten. Her Grace knows nothing, and it will be better that way.'

'As you wish, my lord. I gave you my word. But—what of Carruthers?'

'I have already spoken to him. And that young rip of a nephew of mine will keep silent. I have threatened to tear him limb from limb and roast him over a fire if he lets out the slightest hint.'

Harriet managed a smile at that. 'Did you ring a very great peal over him, my lord!' she asked in almost her old mischievous way.

'Yes, Miss Devenish, I did indeed!'

Harriet heard Lord Richard leave the house some time later and was disappointed that he did not look in upon her again before he departed. But she felt happy that all was well between them again, although Lord Richard had not been his usual lively self and a sort of melancholy had seemed to hang over him. However, she felt comfortable that his anger had been abated.

Harriet had little time for further reflection, however, for no sooner had Lord Richard departed than a ring was heard at the door. Then Lord Talaton's voice was heard in the hall, and the next moment he was with Harriet.

'Miss Devenish!' The viscount came right up to Harriet and caught her hands. 'Miss Devenish, you are quite well today?'

'Indeed I am, my lord, I thank you!'

'You have seen my uncle?'

'Yes. Lord Richard has been here.'

'And did he ring a peal over you?'

'No. Indeed, Lord Richard was rather quiet. Not at all as he usually is. But, I am happy to say, we are quite friends again now.'

Lord Talaton dropped Harriet's hands and fell onto a sofa. 'I am glad to hear that, Miss Devenish, for I should not like to think that you had received anything like the drubbing he gave me!'

'Was your uncle so very angry with you?' Harriet smiled.

'Indeed he was, Miss Devenish! I should not like to go through that half-hour again. I tell you, my uncle has a tongue like a cat-o'-nine-tails when he puts his mind to it! I felt as if I had been flayed alive!' And Lord Talaton looked very gloomy.

'Come, my lord,' Harriet said encouragingly, 'Hard words can never break your bones.'

'When they are such as my uncle spews out, Miss Devenish, I tell you I would rather face a pride of unleashed lions!'

Lord Talaton rose then, and walked about the room quickly, displaying his unease. Harriet watched him, not understanding why he was so uncomfortable now. 'Is there anything amiss, my lord?' she asked at last, when the viscount's perambulations were beginning to wear her nerves to a frazzle.

'No. At least—Well, first, Miss Devenish, my uncle tells me that I must apologize to you. I mean, I understand why I should, and I do so, Miss Devenish, from the bottom of my heart.'

'But—why should you apologize to me, my lord?'

'For taking you to the masquerade. Oh, I quite see now that it was not at all a proper place to take you. I just did not think! We always have so much fun together, and I thought it would be jollier for you than sitting at home, and had quite forgot that—well, only the rather more dubious females go there. You *do* forgive me, dearest Miss Devenish! Say that you do!'

'Of course I do, my lord!'

But though she continued to reassure him, the viscount resumed his pacing.

'Is there something *more* troubling you, my lord?'

Suddenly the young man stopped and faced Harriet

again, a very worried look upon his countenance. Clearly, his mind was whirling about. Then, as clearly, he made up his mind to speak. 'Yes, dash it, there is, Miss Devenish! Something very unfortunate has occurred, and-and-I can not help but feel responsible.'

'I suppose it must have something to do with last night, my lord?'

Lord Talaton nodded unhappily.

'Well, my lord?' Harriet prompted when the viscount showed no disposition to speak further.

'I-I promised my uncle that I would say nothing of it!' Lord Talaton blurted out at last.

'Then you had better remain silent, my lord!' Harriet cried hastily.

'I know!' Lord Talaton looked distressed. 'But—it is all my fault, and—I do wish I could speak of it to someone, for I am in a devilish pucker to know what to do! Oh, I beg your pardon, Miss Devenish, but, really I am at my wits' end.'

'If Lord Richard bade you not speak of it, my lord—'

'If it were anyone other than Rakewell, I would not feel so badly,' Lord Talaton burst out, then looked with horrified eyes at Harriet. 'You must forget I mentioned that name, ma'am!' he cried urgently, clasping her arm.

'Rakewell? Oh, is not that the person who-who-last night—?'

'Yes. He is the one, Miss Devenish.'

'Very well; I have forgot the name, my lord,' Harriet assured the viscount, having, indeed, no wish to remember it.

Lord Talaton remained silent, still holding Harriet's arm, obviously on edge, then abruptly said that he must go.

'But, my lord—you have only just come!'

'I am sorry, Miss Devenish—but—if I remain here any longer, I shall certainly tell you, and you would not wish it, and—I would not wish it when I have promised my uncle.' And Lord Talaton took his leave.

As neither nephew nor uncle had said anything of seeing her again later that day, Harriet felt somewhat deflated when she was alone again, and was thankful when the duchess summoned her to go driving with her.

She saw no more of either Lord Richard or Lord Talaton that day, and the evening was spent quietly, playing back-gammon with the duchess.

The following morning, neither of the men appeared in Mersea Square in the forenoon. Harriet and the duchess partook of their usual light luncheon and were preparing to go out when Lord Richard was announced, his right arm in a sling.

'You have injured yourself?' the duchess demanded, eyeing her son.

'Oh, it is nothing, Mamma,' Lord Richard returned as he bent to kiss his mother's cheek. 'The merest graze, that is all.'

'How did you receive it?'

'A foil slipped,' Lord Richard said dismissively. 'Now, Mamma, Miss Devenish, I called upon Drummond yesterday. I pointed out that it would shortly be a month since Miss Devenish arrived in London, and demanded to know why we have still heard nothing. I told him that if we had still heard nothing within a week—well, by the end of the month—I would begin to make my own enquiries. Either Miss Devenish is entitled to continue to receive an income, or she is not. It is not fair to keep her dangling in this manner. I spoke most forcibly, I can tell you.'

'I make no doubt that you did,' the duchess remarked,

and Harriet turned her head to hide her smile. 'But—supposing we are still in the dark at the end of the month, what exactly would you propose to do?'

'Advertisements in the newspapers; requests for information about the Devenish family—there are many things that may be done. I could see that Drummond understood that I meant business, and I suspect he will not hold out much longer. It is my belief that he knows what is behind this business perfectly well, but has been forbidden to speak. And that the only way to get his principal to release him is to let him know that we have not infinite patience.'

'But—if Mr Drummond does know, I do not see why he should be so unwilling—or rather—why his principal should be so unwilling to let him speak. After all, we are not asking for the name of the principal. Merely whether I shall continue to receive money or not. But, at the beginning of next month, another draft for Miss Bassenthwaite will become due. Mr Drummond—or his principal will have to have made up their minds by then—knowing that I am in London, I mean.'

But to their combined astonishment, Mr Drummond continued silent. Lord Richard visited him again, and then, out of patience, instructed his lawyer to put certain advertisements in the newspapers. Harriet could not but feel uncomfortable, but the duchess begged her not to worry.

During the first week in June, the advertisements had appeared in the London and major provincial newspapers, Harriet was taken to a *fête champêtre* in the grounds of the newly-built residence of the duchess's youngest daughter married to an exceedingly rich gentleman by the name of Fulbrook.

The house in question was a cottage orné, overlooking a lake, and as was customary in such matters, the building was more in the nature of a considerable villa, but with open countryside about it, and a good many trees. Lady Jane Fulbrook, whom Harriet had met once before, had literary aspirations, and had persuaded her husband that a villa near Hampstead Heath, endued with all the pretensions to a pastoral idyll, would assist her in the penning of truly great poetry.

It was extremely agreeable bowling along the lanes to the pleasant village of Hampstead in the duchess's barouche. Lord Richard's arm was not perfectly recovered, or he would have driven himself in his curricle. It was in the latter manner that Lord Talaton betook himself to his aunt's reception.

A very pleasant time was spent wandering through and admiring the spacious rooms of the cottage, and about the newly-gravelled paths. The lawns were, as yet, little more than scythed fields, and much of the new plantings were scarcely more than sprouts, but there was an old woodland bordering the property which provided welcome shade, and the lake itself was old-established, and had its necessary complement of water-lillies and marsh-marigolds brightening its margin.

The duchess's party had already been there some little time when Lord Talaton arrived. He attached himself to Harriet at once, and though Harriet was delighted to see the viscount, she was somewhat disappointed that almost immediately after his arrival, Lord Richard departed, saying that he must go to greet some other friends. They had been enjoying a conversation about modern novels, to which Harriet was greatly addicted, and she had been supporting her claim that Miss Edgeworth produced much more interesting novels than Lord Richard's chosen favourite, Miss Jane Austen.

'But—nothing happens in Miss Austen's novels!' Harriet had cried. 'Why, in *Emma*, there is not one single abduction, or discovery of a dead body, or a cruel step-father—or-or anything!'

Lord Richard had smiled at that. 'You are quite right, Miss Devenish; but Miss Austen does not mean to write of great or very agitating matters. But she has an inimitable eye for what is quietly ridiculous, and a true ear for the niceties of expression.'

'Well, I did not enjoy either *Emma* or *Mansfield Park*,' Harriet had returned. 'Though I will admit that I liked *Pride and Prejudice* well enough.'

It was at that point that Lord Talaton had appeared, and the talk had at once turned into other channels. Lord Talaton never read a book—unless it was the racing calendar. Now the talk was all of the latest *on-dits* about persons in society with whom Harriet was for the most part unacquainted, and very shortly afterwards Lord Richard excused himself. Lord Talaton talked amusingly, and Harriet could not help but laugh, but it crossed her mind for the first time what a rattle Lord Talaton was.

It was not surprising that the young man should offer to drive Harriet back to London in his curricle. 'You will get there a great deal sooner than you would in my grandmamma's carriage, which is a heavy old thing. Besides, Parsons always drives like a snail. And I have a pair of prime new chestnuts—you remember, I told you about them the other day, Miss Devenish! They will fly over the ground, I promise you.'

'I will have to ask Her Grace's permission,' Harriet demurred, mindful of the recent escapade at the Opera House.

'Well, we may easily do that. I am convinced that she

will not raise any objection. And my uncle may accompany her home.'

And indeed the duchess did make no objection, her mind being occupied by her daughter's new toy when the petition was made. Lord Richard was not by at the time. The duchess certainly admonished her grandson to drive carefully, saying that she would hold him entirely responsible if Miss Devenish were not returned to Mersea Square in one piece, but that was all.

And when Lord Richard did hear of the arrangement, he did not look too pleased, but on hearing that the duchess had given her approbation, he made no objection, beyond saying that he did hope his nephew would not drive like a maniac.

'Lord, my uncle does prose so!' Lord Talaton whispered to Harriet when they were alone again. 'He used to be the greatest goer you could imagine, but now I think old age must have smitten him. He is all for prudence and other such dullery now. I can not understand it. It is only these last few weeks that he has been so dismal.'

Harriet protested a little, but more as a matter of form, for she did rather agree with Lord Talaton. Lord Richard, though not so *very* old, did seem overly cautious, and it would be very exciting to be driven fast behind Lord Talaton's thoroughbreds. His equipage was so smart with a liveried tiger behind, and Harriet could not but like to be seen in it. Besides, the road they would follow over the Heath back to London was good and straight; there would be no chance of any misadventure.

However, when they left the drive of Lady Jane's cottage and turned into the main road, there was quite a press of carriages, and it was impossible to make any speed. By dint of much manoeuvring Lord Talaton did manage to pass many of the vehicles, but it was a tedious business, and the chestnuts had no chance to show their paces.

'I had not thought it would be like this!' Lord Talaton complained fretfully. 'Surely not all these people can have been to my aunt's party?'

'Perhaps many of these carriages came out merely for the pleasure of driving. It is, after all, a beautiful day. And we have had a deal of rain lately.'

Lord Talaton continued irritated by the slow progress enforced upon them, and by his inability to show off his cattle's paces to Harriet. When they came out upon the heath itself, therefore, he swung off the main road and turned down a side track.

'This will be a little longer in distance, Miss Devenish; but we shall make far better time. I warrant we shall arrive in Mersea Square a good hour ahead of my grandmother and my uncle.'

The duchess and Lord Richard had left at the same time as Harriet and Lord Talaton, but had fallen far behind them by the time Lord Talaton turned off onto the side road. At first they were able to spank along, and Lord Talaton, now in high good humour, cried out, 'This is more the thing, is not it, Miss Devenish? I told you how it would be! We shall be back in London before them all!'

And Harriet had laughed and agreed, and enjoyed the feel of the wind made by the speed blowing against her cheeks.

But the side road soon turned into little more than a track, and in places the way was obstructed by huge puddles left by the past week's rain. Much of the track was overhung by great trees, under which the ground was very soft, and sometimes it was rather dark, so thick were the leaves. Quite often now Harriet was aware of the tiger clutching the back of the seat.

Harriet saw that all Lord Talaton's irritation was returning, and so she forebore to point out that in spite of the press of the carriages they would have proceeded much faster and in greater comfort along the main road. They bumped along the rutted track and through the puddles, Harriet seeing almost permanently now the tiger's clutching hand out of the corner of her eye. Conversation all but ceased, and there was only an occasional gasp from Harriet as she was thrown about more than usually forcefully, and frequent exclamations of annoyance from Lord Talaton as to the state of the track and the strain it was upon his chestnuts that took its place.

'It grieves me to see them held back like this, Miss Devenish!' Lord Talaton cried more than once. 'It took me scarce an hour to reach my aunt's! I can not think what the turnpike trust is about to let the road fall into such a state!'

Harriet held her tongue and clung to the sideboard more tightly than ever as they went over a more than usually large stone. But now there came the sickening sound of splintering wood, the carriage lurched to one side, and Harriet was all but flung out.

She let out a small scream and clung to the sideboard for all she was worth as the curricle came to rest at a precipitous angle. The horses snorted and strained and Lord Talaton clung to the reins, attempting to hold them.

At last the animals were still. Harriet was half over the side, and Lord Talaton was close up against her, having slid along the seat till he was squashed against her. Now he essayed gingerly to stand up, and somehow managed to scramble to the ground.

'Wh-what has happened, my lord?' Harriet gasped, attempting with one hand to set straight her hat which had been knocked awry. With the other she continued to cling to the sideboard, still fearful of gravity pulling her out.

Luckily the little tiger had managed to jump to the ground uninjured. He had run to the horses' heads while Lord Talaton took a look at his once elegant vehicle. 'The back strap has broken, and the axletree is cracked,' the viscount answered briefly.

Harriet digested this news in silence for some moments, not daring to move, but with her heart sinking into her little slippers. Lord Talaton scowled fearfully as he surveyed the damage to his precious equipage; the tiger's voice hummed as he calmed the still restive horses.

'What must we do then, my lord?' Harriet asked at last.

Lord Talaton looked at her with a rueful grin. 'I am afraid we must walk, Miss Devenish.'

'Walk! To London!'

'No. Of course not! Jack here will take a horse and ride to the next inn where we may hire a carriage. We will walk slowly forwards while he comes back to meet us.' Lord Talaton came round to Harriet's side of the carriage and helped her to clamber down.

She almost fell into Lord Talaton's arms, and once more had to straighten her hat. Meanwhile the tiger was unharnessing the horses, and soon had ridden off to find a conveyance.

'Would you rather wait here, Miss Devenish? Or shall we walk a little along the path?'

'Oh, yes! Pray let us walk a little. It is so dark here under the trees. The sun can scarcely penetrate the foliage.'

'I am exceedingly sorry this had happened, Miss Devenish.'

'Yes, well, it can not be helped.' Harriet was over her

fright now, and beginning to be somewhat irritated by the viscount. After all, this was all his fault. If he had not been so impatient and they had stuck to the main road, this mishap would never have happened.

She started to walk quite briskly, stepping from stone to stone to avoid the mud. Lord Talaton hurried beside her, regretting the accident to his curricle. Harriet would have been better pleased if his lordship had dwelt longer on the inconvenience and discomfort to herself.

They walked for some time with only desultory conversation. The track emerged from the wood and Harriet felt better and consequently more charitable when she was in warm sunshine once more. But then they came to a fork in the track, and both hesitated as to which path to take.

'If we go to the right, Miss Devenish, we will come upon the main road again very shortly, I feel sure,' Lord Talaton announced at last.

Harriet was anxious to get back to other carriages and people, and accordingly they turned in that direction.

But after some moments, the track divided again, and it was impossible to tell which way the tiger might have taken. Wheel tracks and hoof prints were everywhere, and none looked newer than the rest.

Harriet began to feel tired. After all, she was not shod for country walking, and every stone seemed to cut through her slippers, bruising her feet.

'Do you think the road can be much farther, my lord?' she asked wearily when they had been walking for what seemed a very long time.

The track they were following was broad, and appeared to be well-used, but they came upon no other travellers. A great many clumps of gorse hid a wide view from their sight.

'I felt certain that we should have come upon the road before now,' Lord Talaton returned, looking a little worried. 'I fear we have missed our way.'

'Oh!' Harriet groaned, wondering how much farther she could go. 'Surely not, my lord!'

'Let us rest a little Miss Devenish. It is very hot still in the sunshine.'

Harriet glanced up at the sky and saw somewhat uneasily that the sun was making its way down to the horizon. She had visions of their being benighted here on this inhospitable common. But, time or no time, she would have to rest.

Accordingly she sank down on a tussock and eased her toes. Never before had she had such sore feet. She had walked quite a lot in Cumberland, and the walking had not been easy, but then she had worn boots fit for the purpose, not little thin slippers such as she wore now.

They had been sitting there for a few minutes, saying little except reassurances mainly for their own benefit that they must come upon the main road soon, when the sound of a carriage came distinctly to their ears.

'That will be Jack now!' Lord Talaton cried excitedly, jumping up and looking eagerly about him.

But the carriage was not approaching from in front of them, but from the side, and when it came into view it was seen to be drawn not by Lord Talaton's chestnuts, but by a pair of bays, and the coachman was not Lord Talaton's tiger, but a stranger.

The chaise passed them without stopping, but a short distance past them it drew to a halt. The coachman got down, spoke to his master at the door of the chaise, then came back to them and said very civilly, 'My master asks if he may be of service to you?'

Lord Talaton hesitated for a moment, but looked down at Harriet's weary face, then said very gratefully that he would be glad to be taken to the main road where they expected to meet their own conveyance. The servant assured them that his master would be only too willing to assist them in this manner, and returned to the carriage and spoke to its occupant while Lord Talaton helped Harriet to her feet.

"What a stroke of luck, Miss Devenish, that a gentleman should be passing this way! We will soon be at the inn, and then back to London.'

'But your tiger—where can he be?'

'Oh, he will find his way home soon enough when he discovers that we are gone. We will leave a message with the innkeeper.'

They came up to the carriage now. The coachman was standing beside the door with the step down. He helped Harriet inside. The curtains were drawn and it was dark in the vehicle, and Harriet blinked as she came in out of the light, quite unable for the moment to see the occupant.

Then she heard a scuffle behind her and a cry from Lord Talaton. The door was slammed shut, there came the sound of the coachman scrambling up onto the box, and in a moment the vehicle set off, first at a fast trot, then at a canter.

Harriet herself nearly fell on her nose, so unexpected was the vehicle's sudden movement. Now that the door was closed, it was almost black inside the vehicle, and Harriet was seized with terror from top to toe. She let out a strangled little cry as her clutching hand met what felt like human flesh, and she fell onto the seat, drawing herself as far away from her unseen companion as she could.

'Who are you, sir?' she managed to utter breathlessly.

'Where are you taking me? What have you done to Lord Talaton?'

'Pray do not be alarmed, Miss Devenish,' an odious and all—too—familiar voice oozed now. 'It *is* Miss Devenish, is it not?''

With a heart that plumeted like lead into her boots, Harriet recognized the voice as belonging to the man who had tried to ravish her at the Opera masquerade: the man Lord Richard had called Rakewell.

Six

As she heard the hateful voice, Harriet drew in her breath with a strangled shriek, and cringed still further into her corner. Fear took her in its toils and her mind felt as if glue had been poured into its works so that the wheels would not turn and it refused to function.

Dimly she heard Rakewell's voice through the suffocating darkness. 'Come, my dear; there is no need for you to alarm yourself so. You will not be harmed.' The voice was silky and threatening.

'Wh-what have you done with Lord Talaton?' Harriet got out in a tiny voice.

'Oh, he will have a few scratches from the gorse bushes, that is all. Perhaps a black eye. It depends where Jackson got him. But you need not worry about him.' Harriet felt a hand fumbling for her arm. 'That young blade would only have spoilt a pleasant tête-à-tête.'

'Don't touch me!' Harriet shrieked. 'Keep away from me! If you touch me I will scream!'

'And who do you think will hear you in this desolate spot? I assure you, Miss Devenish, we are far away from any road here. There is no chance of any unwanted interference this time. It really is a remarkable piece of luck, my coming upon you like that! I confess I was very much astonished when I saw who it was I was passing.'

'H-how do you know my name, sir?'

'After our little—misunderstanding—the previous evening, Miss Devenish, it was not difficult to find out the name of the young lady for whom Lord Richard Halton showed such—gallant solicitude! I have seen you several times before, my dear. You are his lordship's ward, I collect?'

Harriet remained mute, and the hand clutching her arm shook her a little, none too gently.

'Pray answer, my dear,' the odious voice continued; 'I am in the mood for a little conversation.'

'Yes, I am,' Harriet answered shortly, fearing worse violence if she did not do as she was bid, and the fingers grasping her arm were already digging into her flesh most painfully.

'That is better. And—where do you come from, Miss Devenish?'

'From Cumberland.'

'Cumberland!'

Still gripping her arm, the dreadful man continued to question her: how long she had been his lordship's ward, why the circumstance had come about. Harriet's eyes grew accustomed to the gloom, and soon she was able to make out the shape of the wretch who was abducting her. She recognized the thin mouth, but the glittering eyes looked less frightening now than they had when seen behind the domino, and accordingly Harriet's first terror began to recede a little.

Besides, if she were able to hold the man's attention by conversation, perhaps she would be able to put off any more disagreeable attentions. Accordingly, she spread herself in her answers, growing suddenly quite loquacious. She spoke of her early years with her parents; the great house they had inhabited and which she dimly remembered; her beautiful mother, gentle and ailing, who had soon followed her dead husband to the grave with a broken heart. Harriet herself was quite affected, and might have been even more so, had she not had the sense to pull herself together, and while she was answering the questions, revolve in her mind how she might escape.

Even if she did somehow manage to get out of the carriage, she had no doubt that the coachman would certainly help to recapture her; besides, if she merely flung herself out while the vehicle was moving, she might quite well break an arm or a leg, or injure herself in some other way which would effectively stop her escape, and put her in a worse pass than she was already. No; she could not like the idea of flinging herself out of the chaise at all! She must think of something better.

Oh, how she wished Lord Richard were with her! He would know what to do! For the first time since it had happened all those weeks ago, she recalled how expeditiously Lord Richard had dealt with the highwaymen who had waylaid them on the Cumberland road. True, she had not seen exactly what had happened, being shut up in the trunk, but she had heard plainly enough. And then—Lord Richard had rescued her from the loathsome Mr Rakewell once before. He had reduced him to an inert bag of bones in no time at all. Harriet smiled as she saw in her mind's eye Mr Rakewell slipping slowly down the wall of the—as she now knew it to have been—Royal box.

She had no doubt at all that Lord Richard would act now

in the same swift and effective manner. Oh! How she wished he were here!

'Your family must have been one of considerable wealth, my dear,' Mr Rakewell said now in a reflective sort of voice.

'Of course it was!' Harriet returned.

'And so—you are quite an heiress, Miss Devenish?'

Harriet heard the words with surprise. Such an idea had never occurred to her before. She had never expected anything more than a continued allowance. But now the idea was put into words, Harriet could not help but gasp a little. It might—indeed, it *could* be possible! An heiress! Harriet savoured the thought.

The hand clutching her shook her arm again. 'Well, Miss Devenish?'

'I have—very important connections, sir. They will know how to act when they find out what you have done.'

'Ah, but Miss Devenish, they will not find out until it is too late.' Mr Rakewell began chuckling then, an odious, direful sound. 'Well, my dear Miss Devenish,' he continued in his disgusting, drawling voice, 'you must admit that this is a much more convenient place in which to get to know each other than the previous venue. There is no fear of the noble lord bursting in upon us now. Yes—we shall have plenty of time. I think, Miss Devenish, I am going to enjoy the next few days very much indeed.'

'What do you mean, sir?' Harriet demanded as bravely as she could, but fear taking hold of her again.

'It is a long journey back to your native county, Miss Devenish.'

'I do not understand you, sir!'

'Gretna, I collect, is very close to the Cumberland border.'

'Gretna!'

'Why, yes, Miss Devenish! I confess that at first I had not realized what a prize you were. I thought merely to—*annoy*—his lordship. But—I see now that you have unsuspected charms of your own!' And Mr Rakewell's leering face came closer to Harriet's.

Pressed hard against the squabs of the carriage, Harriet sought for some means of defence with every ounce of her mental ability. Her mind was working again now, clarified by fear this time. One arm was in Mr Rakewell's grasp, but the other was at liberty, and as Mr Rakewell's face came closer to her two, Harriet screwed her left hand into a fist and suddenly punched it into the man's face for all she was worth.

Mr Rakewell let out a shriek of his own now, released Harriet and put both hands to his nose, 'She-devil!' he moaned, as he fumbled in his pocket. At last he drew out his handkerchief and clapped it to his face, but not before Harriet had had the satisfaction of seeing blood running down his chin.

Harriet was frightened by what she had done, fearing that Mr Rakewell might use even greater force against her, but to her relief the dreadful man now moved away from her and let up the blind on one side of the carriage.

'You have spoilt my waistcoat!' he cried in a muffled voice after a moment's inspection of his person. 'Look!'

And Harriet saw that a few drops of blood had fallen onto the pristine yellow silk.

'And it is but new on today!'

'Then, you should have behaved like a gentleman, and it would not have happened!' Harriet said severely now. She felt quite brave again, for Mr Rakewell seemed oddly deflated now.

'Let me tell you, ma'am, you are no lady!' Mr Rakewell returned, his voice still complaining. 'You are all of a piece with your precious guardian! Boxing like a man! I have never heard the like! Deuce take it, I'd give a deal to call you out as I did Halton. He did not escape so easily! A ball in his shoulder was what he got for his pains!'

Harriet stared across the coach, her heart racing. 'You mean—you fought a duel with Lord Richard?'

'Of course I did, you little devil! How else do you think he got that wound?'

'But he said—' Harriet stopped. So, Lord Richard had not been wounded practising fencing as he had said, but had been called out by this man! Why! He might have been killed! It came to her as a flash of lightning just how she would have felt if anything had happened to Lord Richard.

'Well, whatever he said, it was not the truth, for I put that shot into him,' Mr Rakewell said now, rather sulkily.

Harriet screwed both her hands into fists now, and felt a great urge to belabour Mr Rakewell. 'I suppose you wish you had killed him!' Harriet fumed back.

'I am not such a fool, Miss Devenish! But I paid him back for his impertinence.'

Mr Rakewell then subsided into his corner, muttering and patting his injured nose, while Harriet sat back in her own corner, subdued now by the self-knowledge which had so abruptly come to her. She hardly heard Mr Rakewell, and looked through the window, certainly not absorbing what they passed.

And even when the coach slowed down preparatory to drawing to a halt, still Harriet could not make up her mind to act decisively herself. She had an unshakeable confidence that somehow Lord Richard would find her and rescue her, just as he had done before. How he should manage this, she could not think, but that it would happen, she had not the least doubt.

The carriage halted at last, the door was opened, and the step let down, Jackson standing foursquare in the doorway. Peering out, Harriet saw that she was at the front door to a large mansion-house, and that a footman was hovering in the background.

'Go on! Get out, Miss Devenish!' Mr Rakewell demanded petulantly. 'And bread and water for you, ma'am, while you cool your heels!'

At that, Jackson reached into the carriage and pulled her out. Harriet tugged against his hand indignantly, but naturally she was no match for the big man. 'Let me go, sir!' she cried, but of course to no avail.

Instead the coachman proceeded to drag her into the house. Harriet had little time to notice more than that the house was not very old, and looked very fine indeed, before she was dragged up the short flight of steps to the front door and past an elegant balustrade edging a terrace in front of the house.

Behind her she heard Mr Rakewell's footsteps. The coachman paused in the cool hall, and Harriet turned to see her abductor. He was still dabbing his nose tenderly.

Suddenly Harriet could not restrain a laugh. The appearance of Mr Rakewell was almost woebegone. The spots besmirching his yellow waistcoat had now turned a dull brown, and there was a smear of blood also on the hand clasped to his face. Compared with the man of such evil intentions as he had been a short time before, his present dropping demeanour was too much for the girl.

Why! Mr Rakewell was nothing but a bully, and if one stood up to bullies, even a woman might save herself.

Now Mr Rakewell entered the spacious, light hall, furnished with a quantity of very pretty modern satinwood pieces. He looked sourly at Harriet's merry face and scowled. 'Upstairs with her, Jackson. And make certain my guest does not escape.'

Without a word, the coachman pulled Harriet forward and up the stairs. The man's face was impassive as he clutched her by the arm, his grip unyielding, and Harriet stumbled a little as she was drawn inexorably forward.

But when they had passed the first floor and were out of Mr Rakewell's sight, she whispered urgently, 'Oh, pray let me go, Jackson! You will be well rewarded for it, I promise you! My friends will see to it that you are very well rewarded!'

But for all the notice the man took of her, she might as well have remained silent. He continued to draw her up the staircase beside him to the next floor. There, he crossed the landing, still in silence, opened a door, and thrust the girl inside without once looking at her. Then he closed the door, turned the key in the lock, and the next moment Harriet heard his footsteps descending the staircase once more.

Anger now took the place of fright and Harriet hammered on the door. 'Let me out! Let me out!' she roared.

But the footsteps faded away, and then an uncanny silence descended upon the big house.

For some moments, Harriet continued to hammer on the door, but no-one took any notice of her, and her knuckles became quickly sore. So she stopped and turned to survey her prison. Seeing bars across the window she guessed that she must be in the nursery. Swiftly crossing the room to look out of the window, she saw far below her a courtyard and stables, and beyond that a farmyard; and beyond that again parkland dotted with trees. Clearly she was imprisoned in a room at the back of the house.

She tried the window, and to her relief it opened quite easily, and she drew in great gasps of fresh air. It was very hot at the top of the house, and the room was stuffy, and the girl felt relief as the cooler air struck her cheek. It was not yet dusk, but the sun was sinking, and was already turning into a great orange ball hanging in the sky. Below her she saw a maid cross the courtyard carrying a pail. Harriet shouted as loudly as she could, but the servant did not glance up.

When the servant disappeared from sight, Harriet turned to survey the room itself. There was a cradle, and a truckle-bed for the nurse on one side. In the middle of the room stood a deal table and a couple of chairs, and near the door, opposite the window, stood a chest-of-drawers. A rag rug completed the furnishings of the room.

Seized again with anger, Harriet returned to the door and pounded upon it. 'Let me out, Mr Rakewell! Let me out!'

But she was answered only by silence. Fuming with indignation Harriet drew one of the chairs to the window and stared out into the park, her chin cupped in her hand. As she sat there, it came to her that she felt exceedingly hungry, and she hoped that Mr Rakewell would think to send her food. She recalled what he had said about bread and water, and grimaced to herself; but as time went by, even that dry fare began to take on the lusciousness of a good beef pie.

But no-one came near her, and the house maintained its strange quiet.

After a long time, Harriet got up again and went to hammer on the door. She shouted and banged, but dispiritedly, as thought she expected no answer. The sun was falling rapidly to the horizon, and when she stopped, Harriet went over to the truckle-bed and took off her hat and lay down. For the first time she began to feel sorry for herself, and tears of self-pity oozed out of her eyes and slid down her cheeks and onto the pillow. If only she had some food, she would feel much better. She never did feel her best when she was hungry.

And for the first time she had doubts that Lord Richard would arrive to rescue her. After all, how should he know where to look for her? She might be anywhere in England.

She wondered what Mr Rakewell intended to do with her. He had said something about Gretna—but—there were many things he might do before they reached that distant Scottish village. She did not think she was exactly frightened of him any more. When he had been covered by the domino at the masquerade, he had looked frightening and evil, but now that she had seen him dressed normally, he was no longer a figure of terror. He was only a dandified bully, who had been upset by the sight of blood spoiling his waistcoat.

Harriet smiled grimly at the recollection of her abductor's dismay; but commonsense told her that she did not know enough of Mr Rakewell to judge how he might behave in the future. That he was vindictive she had no doubt, and though he might not be prepared to endure another thump upon the nose, it occurred to her that he might get Jackson to deal with her, and she did not think the coachman would flinch from anything.

Lying in the quickly gathering darkness, Harriet began to pray very urgently that rescue—preferably in the shape of Lord Richard Halton—would come to her very quickly.

It was a long time later that Harriet woke up. It was quite dark now except for a pale rectangle that was the window, and for some seconds Harriet wondered where she was. Somewhere in the distance she could hear shouting, and the sound of many feet running, and she wondered what on earth it could be that would cause the duchess's servant to behave in such an extraordinary fashion.

But then the recollection of where she was came back to her, and in that instant she heard clearly what was being shouted. She was not mistaken when she realized that it was her own name. In a flash, she was fully awake, as effectively as if a bucket of icy water had been thrown over her, and at once she jumped off the truckle-bed and ran across the room to the door.

'I am here, my lord! Upstairs! In the nursery!' she screamed, beating on the door with her fists.

Above all the other noises came the pounding of feet on the staircase. 'Harriet! Where are you, Harriet?'

'Here, my lord! I am here! In the nursery!' Harriet screamed again.

It was lucky that the key had been left in the lock. There was no need this time for Lord Richard to hurl himself against the door to break it open. He had but to turn the key, as simply and as easily as he might open a locked drawer in his own home, and the next moment, Harriet had flung herself into his arms.

'Miss Devenish! Are you all right? Have you been harmed?' Lord Richard demanded, holding her away for a moment to look at her in the dim light that came up the stairs from the candles below.

'No, no! I am quite well. But, oh! I am so very hungry!'

'Oh, Miss Devenish! You—nonsensical child!' And Lord Richard clasped her to him again.

'Oh, my lord!' Harriet wept a little with relief now. 'You

have saved me again! 'She drew back to peer at him. 'I was certain—I *knew* you would!'

'Oh, my dear Miss Devenish!' Lord Richard said, a little shakily, she thought. 'What have you been about? I thought you had known from the last time what kind of man Rakewell was! Why did you go off with him?'

'I did not, my lord!' Harriet cried indignantly, springing back. 'I had not the least chance to do otherwise!'

'But where was Talaton? Why did he do nothing?'

'He was knocked down by the coachman, my lord! He had no chance to exert himself! While he was floundering in the gorse bushes, the coachman had jumped onto the box and sprung the horses!'

'I noticed he looked somewhat scratched about the face when he came to me! But he was hardly coherent, and I did not take time to question him too narrowly. He was in the duece of a pucker when he told me that you had been abducted—and by Rakewell!'

'But—how did he know that? How did you know where to look for me, my lord?'

But before Lord Richard could answer, there were voices from below demanding to know if the young lady had been found, and Lord Richard shouted back, leaning over the banister rail, and said that she was quite safe, and then he took Harriet's arm, and together they went downstairs. In the candlelight in the hall, Mr Rakewell was standing, looking very sulky, and scowling furiously, and guarded by two burly fellows in red waistcoats, one holding each arm.

Harriet, driven by she knew not what imp, could not help saying with a certain smug satisfaction and a pert smile, 'His lordship, I thank heaven, has arrived to disturb you again, sir!'

Mr Rakewell looked baleful, and muttered something under his breath which Harriet did not catch. At a nod from Lord Richard, the two redbreasts hustled Mr Rakewell towards the door.

'I'll be even with you for this, Halton!' that person cried, his voice high-pitched with anger. 'I'll pay you for your interference!'

But he had time for nothing more, for he was bundled outside, and the door swung to upon him, effectively shutting off his protests and imprecations.

Lord Richard turned to Harriet and smiled. 'Well, a spell in gaol should cool his heels for him. And then, I think, we must persuade him that a spell upon the continent would be the best for his health.'

'Oh, yes, my lord! I should like that of all things!' Harriet cried. 'I should feel a good deal more comfortable if I thought Mr Rakewell were out of England! I fear I should never feel safe, and should be looking behind me all the time!'

'I think we might very well manage that,' Lord Richard returned, a grim look coming into his eye.

'But still you have not told me, my lord,' Harriet cried, clinging to Lord Richard's arm, 'how you came to find me. How did you know where to come?'

'Oh, it was not at all difficult, Miss Devenish. That normally addle-pated nephew of mine for once used his head, and, by great good fortune, recognized the horses. They had come up at Tattersall's, scarce a se'night ago, it seems, and, Talaton being Talaton, he could call to mind not only their price and their bloodline, but the seller and the new owner also.

'So, when he told me what happened and at what spot, *and* that he was certain that the horses were the bays Rakewell had purchased such a short time ago. I knew that your abductor must indeed be Rakewell. His father built this house outside London, Miss Devenish, and Rakewell is known to use it at times. So, having alerted the Runners, we came straight here. But, are you quite certain that you have not been harmed, Miss Devenish?' And Lord Richard looked down at her with very anxious eyes.

'Oh, not in the least, my lord, I promise you! Certainly, in the carriage, Mr Rakewell did try to—that is—' Here Harriet blushed, then gave a little chuckle. 'Well, it ended by my punching him in the nose, and it bled on his new waistcoat, and, after that, well, Mr Rakewell did not seem very interested in anything but in staunching the flow.'

'You—what, Miss Devenish!' Lord Richard exclaimed with a laugh. ' 'Pon my soul, it seems to me that there is not all that need to rush to your aid! You seem quite capable of defending yourself—most adequately!'

'Well, I am very glad you did come, my lord! It was not at all agreeable, and Mr Rakewell might *not* have been so easy to keep under control! And do you know, my lord! He wanted to call me out! As he did you, my lord, I collect! Oh! Why did not you tell me?' Harriet ended accusingly.

'So, he told you that, did he? Well, it was the merest graze. And if I had said anything, quite apart from what the law might have done, my mamma would have been in a pucker, and really, it was but a scratch.'

Harriet looked at Lord Richard searchingly. 'Was it really nothing, my lord? I saw you wincing often.'

'Of course it was, you nonsensical child! Did I look in the least feverish?'

'But—you did not drive to Hampstead! Your arm was too painful!'

'One does not hammer away at a bruise on purpose, Miss Devenish; I hope I have learnt sense enough for that!' Lord Richard returned briskly. Then he added, 'Well, we had better return to London as soon as we can, and then you may have some supper. That will soon put you to rights!'

Harriet felt disappointed somehow that Lord Richard was still treating her as a rather naughty child. She gave him a reproachful look.

But it is doubtful that his lordship saw it. There came the sound of carriage wheels approaching outside, and Lord Richard went to the door and looked out.

'Ah, here is Porter now. I told him to bring a cloak for you, Miss Devenish. There is a chill wind now that the sun is down.'

'Thank you. But I feel very warm,' Harriet said in a small voice, disappointed still by Lord Richard's brusque answer to her solicitous enquiry.

But Lord Richard did not hear that either. He had turned to speak to the remaining Runners in the hall, then turned back to Harriet. 'They have not found the coachman, I collect, Miss Devenish, but the other servants are being questioned now. Have you any complaint to make against any of them?'

Harriet shook her head. 'None of them came near me, my lord. It was the coachman who took me upstairs, and who punched Lord Talaton. I know nothing ill of any of the others.'

'Well, let us be on our way then, Miss Devenish. I confess I am itching to get back to London!'

'Why is that, my lord?'

'Because I mean to give that addle-pated nephew of mine the drubbing of his life!'

114

'He complained about the rake-down you gave him before, my lord!' Harriet smiled. 'But, this time, Lord Talaton could do nothing! He was knocked down and we were off in a trice! Really, you should not blame him!'

'Not blame him! Miss Devenish, I am not referring to his inability to keep you from being abducted. That I understand well enough, and in any case, I have never had any doubts as to Talaton's courage. No! What I shall complain of is his leaving the high road. Had he not done that, you would have been surrounded by other carriages, Miss Devenish, and Rakewell would have had no chance to take you. He must have thanked his guardian angel for the luck which had put you in such a position, and by which he was almost enabled to get even with me. Why *did* you leave the turnpike, Miss Devenish?'

'There were so many carriages upon it, we could move but slowly, my lord, and Lord Talaton thought we would make better progress along a less-used track.'

'And you ended up being abducted by Rakewell! Well, I advise you in future, Miss Devenish, stick to the main road. It will not lead you astray.'

Harriet nodded agreement ruefully, and Lord Richard led her out to his own carriage, which Porter had now stationed before the front door, and helped her inside then climbed in after her. He insisted upon draping her cloak about her, then settled himself on the seat opposite her.

It was then that Harriet remembered her hat. 'Oh! I have left it in the nursery, my lord!'

But the carriage had already started to move.

'Do you really want us to turn back?'

'No. It does not matter, my lord. I-I think also it would not look its best after all it has gone through.'

'And—I dare say you will be able to find an even prettier

115

one, Miss Devenish. By the way, I do not think I mentioned it, but—you looked particularly fetching today.'

'Thank you, my lord,' Harriet whispered, suddenly shy, but suddenly exceedingly happy. She gazed at him across the carriage and saw that his teeth gleamed as he smiled at her.

Harriet was glad for the darkness which hid her abruptly crimsoning cheeks.

Seven

Two days after the *fête champêtre* and Harriet's temporary abduction by Mr Rakewell, Lord Richard came to Mersea Square early in the morning with news from his lawyer. Mr Harcombe asked if his lordship would wait upon him at twelve noon to discuss the question of the newspaper advertisements.

'Oh, my lord, there is news at last!' Harriet cried excitedly, delighted by this turn in events.

'It seems so, Miss Devenish. And of course you must come with me, and my mother also.'

The three of them arrived punctually in the Strand, Harriet herself in a high state of agitation: a mixture of fear and excitement. Quite what she should fear she had no idea; if it turned out that there was to be no more money for her, then she would find work. And now that she was no longer alone in the world, but had friends upon whom she was sure she would depend for help, she might well find a very agreeable situation. Besides, she was confident that the duchess would never throw her out into the street.

And if the very worst should happen—well, she was convinced that she might return to Miss Bassenthwaite and teach in the school in Cumberland. Of that, she had no doubt. Had not Miss Bassenthwaite ever been kindness itself to her?

But, superstitiously, Harriet kept her fingers crossed that this would not be the result of the visit to Mr Harcombe.

The lawyer turned out to be a dry, plump little man with piercing grey eyes, and a surprisingly puckish smile. 'Well, and so this is the young lady!' he exclaimed when Harriet was presented. 'Believe me, I am delighted to meet you, my dear Miss Devenish!'

And Mr Harcombe did indeed look so genuinely delighted that Harriet felt immediately reassured, and was certain that she was to hear good news.

But Mr Harcombe's profession was too much for him, and in spite of his obvious goodwill, he was unable to come to the point at once, but had to give—at very great length—explanations of the actions he had taken at Lord Richard's instigation.

But at last he did come to the heart of the matter, and he turned a beaming face upon Harriet. 'The upshot of all this is, dear Miss Devenish, that I am in the happy position of being able to tell you that your allowance will be continued. You will receive over the year, in four quarterly installments, the sum of five hundred pounds. This, it is believed, will enable you, now that you have left school and are to come out into the world, to live in some—creditable manner.'

'Five hundred pounds!' Harriet repeated, much astonished. 'But—that is a fortune!'

'It is sufficient, certainly, for you to live in a respectable manner,' Mr Harcombe agreed. 'However, I must tell you that upon your marriage, your allowance will cease. A suitable sum will be provided for your dowry, but from then on, no further income may be expected.

'Oh!' Harriet exclaimed; 'I was certain all along that my benefactor would continue kind. Oh, is not it a noble sum!' And she turned beaming to the duchess and Lord Richard.

'A—princely sum, we may say, Miss Devenish,' Mr Harcombe beamed before the duchess or Lord Richard had said a word; then suddenly he seemed to be afflicted by a cough, and cleared his throat very loudly.

The duchess and her son were now warm in their congratulations, happy for Harriet.

When the first flush of enthusiastic pleasure had died away, Harriet turned to Mr Harcombe again. 'And can you tell me, sir, to whom I am indebted? Whom may I thank for this—munificence?'

Mr Harcombe put his fingers together. 'There will be no need for thanks, Miss Devenish. Your—benefactor—does not require them. Instructions have been given that in future you are to receive the drafts instead of Miss-er-Bassenthwaite, I think it was. As I say, they will arrive quarterly. And Midsummer Day will soon be here, Miss Devenish, and with it your first quarter's allowance.' Suddenly he shot her an almost fatherly look. 'Until then, ma'am, perhaps you may be in need of a little small change to tide you over?'

'Oh, no, I thank you sir!' Harriet said quickly. 'I am quite well provided. I still have fifteen shillings and fourpence!'

'That is indeed a goodly sum, Miss Devenish,' Mr Harcombe smiled.

Now Lord Richard spoke. '*I* can not be entirely satisfied, Harcombe. You are working for me, please remember. As you so rightly said, it was I who put these enquiries in hand. What I would wish to know is, what guarantee has Miss Devenish that the money will continue to arrive? Surely it would be more satisfactory if Miss Devenish were to have a sum laid down which might be invested to produce the income specified?'

'I am not at liberty to discuss this matter, my lord,' Mr Harcombe said slowly. I regret it, but—'

'But—you act for me, I would remind you!'

'I act also—for Miss Devenish's benefactor, my lord.'

Lord Richard stared and did not look too pleased. 'But, this is even less satisfactory, Harcombe. I do not think I can accept this arrangement.'

Mr Harcombe paused before replying, adjusting the items on his desk, already placed in meticulous order, a fraction of an inch one way or the other. After some moments, he said slowly, 'I understand your lordship's feelings entirely, but—I can only say that—I have acted for Miss Devenish's benefactor for many years.'

'Your firm has been the Halton family solicitor for many years!' Lord Richard retorted quite heatedly.

Mr Harcombe spread his hands. 'I deeply regret, my lord . . . '

It was the duchess who broke in now and brought this rather fruitless exchange to a close. 'I think Miss Devenish and I must leave now, Richard. Perhaps you would be kind enough to escort us? Mr Harcombe, I am sure Miss Devenish would wish to thank you for the excellent news you have been able to give her. Not unnaturally, up to now, Miss Devenish has been very unsettled, not knowing if—if she could expect any continuance of her allowance.'

'I am delighted, Your Grace, to have been the bearer of such excellent news.'

Harriet thanked Mr Harcombe once more, and the party

left, with Lord Richard still seeming far from satisfied. When they were in the barouche again, Lord Richard said frowning, 'I can not like it that Harcombe should be acting for both sides. Why did not you let me press him, Mamma? I should have got something from him in the end.'

'I rather think not, my dear,' the duchess returned. 'Indeed, I am convinced of it. Harcombe and his firm have been our solicitors for as long as I can remember, and during that time I can not think of one occasion when we have had cause to complain of his conduct. Should not we expect him to behave in the same manner by his other clients?'

'Of course, Mamma. But my point is that he should not be acting for both sides.

'It may well be, that in this case, Mr Harcombe had had no choice, Richard.'

'Then he should have told me before of his double interest!'

'Perhaps when you went to see him about Miss Devenish's affairs, he did not know of it.'

Lord Richard grunted. 'Then, when he did know, he should have told Miss Devenish's benefactor, whoever he is, that he could not act for him in this case.'

'Richard,' the duchess said very patiently now, masking a mild irritation, 'I have known Mr Harcombe a good deal longer than you, and I have not the slightest doubt of his probity. I am quite prepared to accept that Mr Harcombe has acted for the best in what was for him, most probably, an exceedingly delicate situation. After all, we have what we have wanted from the beginning: the assurance that Miss Devenish will receive an allowance so long as she needs one. And we have that assurance, and the further assurance that the allowance is indeed more than adequate.'

'Oh, yes, indeed!' Harriet cried. 'I had not expected anything like that.'

But Lord Richard did not seem to share her joy. He still frowned, and said, 'I do not understand you, Mamma. How should these enquiries have been delicate?'

But the duchess did not answer, merely glancing at Harriet whose face was turned away, her attention having been caught by some street acrobats as they drove along Pall Mall. The duchess then looked back at her son, and shook her head and frowned in a manner to indicate that the subject should be dropped.

And it was, and the remainder of the journey passed in desultory conversation about a theatrical performance in the Haymarket, and whether Lord Richard meant to drive up to Newmarket for the races later in the week.

Back in Mersea Square, Harriet went to her room to take off her shawl and bonnet, and did not see Lord Richard detain his mother and draw her into the small salon. When Harriet came downstairs again, she hesitated a moment, wondering where the other two were, then she saw that the door of the small salon was slightly ajar and crossed quickly to it. As she approached, she heard Lord Richard's voice say very quietly, 'But are not you going to tell Harriet of your suspicions?'

'I think it better not to,' the duchess's voice returned, also whispering. 'Clearly it is wished that the matter should still remain a secret. And, in any case, my idea is quite without any proof. It is a suspicion, merely.'

'Certainly it would explain everything. The anonymous payments. The continuing allowance. The lack of any final provision—it is only too well known what debts there are in that quarter—such a sum as would provide five hundred pounds per annum, would mean a capital of some seventeen thousand pounds or thereabouts, and would be quite beyond the gentleman, I am sure.'

'Exactly.'

Harriet could not help overhearing the first part of this conversation. She knew, of course, that the right course was for her to open the salon door firmly and enter, or depart. But on hearing her own name, the temptation to stay for more was too great, and she stayed.

There was a pause now in the murmur of quiet voices from the salon, and Harriet put up her hand preparatory to pushing open the door. But the next moment she stayed her hand; the conversation was continued, but on a different tack.

'What is to become of Harriet?' Lord Richard asked.

'How do you mean?'

'I asked you to look after her—as an emergency. Already she has been here over a month. I had not thought it would be permanent.'

'I am only too happy to have the child here. She is a companion to me.'

'It is very good of you, Mamma, but I can not like it that you should be encumbered—'

'Harriet is no encumbrance, Richard. I tell you, I like to have her here.'

'But I feel responsible—'

'Because of the silly joke about your being her guardian? Well, there is no need for you to concern yourself farther if you do not like it. *I* shall be glad to keep Harriet with me. You may wash your hands of her.'

Lord Richard's voice said irritably, 'It was only as a result of my stupid curiosity, and I did not mean to drag you into it. With five hundred pounds per annum, Harriet would be able to set herself up—'

'Pray do not talk nonsense, Richard! A young girl like that—entirely alone? And where should she set herself up?' There was silence for a moment, then the duchess's voice continued, 'Would you be happy with such an arrangement? *I* should not. I have grown fond of Harriet, and am only too happy to be responsible for her, whatever you may feel.'

'Deuce take it, Mamma! I feel responsible also! Oh, I beg your pardon, but—'

'And you would be rid of the responsibility?'

'Of course not, Mamma! I think you know that.'

But Harriet did not hear Lord Richard's last remark. Stricken to her inmost core by what she had just overheard, Harriet crept back to her own room, and there collapsed in a crumpled heap on the floor, weeping bitterly. Lord Richard did not want her! She was an—encumbrance! A burden! An-an incubus! The duchess was kind, and Harriet was very grateful to her for that kindness. But—it was Lord Richard's kindness she wanted.

She recognized that now. How blind she had been not to have seen it before. She had had an inkling of it when she had been abducted by that dreadful Mr Rakewell. Then she had depended upon Lord Richard to rescue her. And, when he had come, she had felt very sweet relief.

But, even then, she had not realized—had not known—how she really felt. For all the time she had been flirting with Lord Talaton, it had been Lord Richard who had supported her, who had come to her rescue, upon whom she had depended, as upon a safe rock. But, now that rock had been cut away, and only now did she understand how much she needed him.

At the very moment—almost at the very moment—that she had been given security—again, a circumstance which

124

had been brought about by Lord Richard's exertions on her behalf—she was suddenly flung into the depths of despair. Knowing that Lord Richard wished to be rid of her turned all her pleasure into dross.

There floated into Harriet's mind then, the vision of Lady Charlotte Logan as she had seen her speaking to Lord Richard at the *fête champêtre*, gazing up smiling into his face. Against such competition, what chance had Harriet Devenish ever stood?

Harriet had been in the room for some time when a maid came with an enquiry from the duchess as to whether all was well.

'Is-is Her Grace alone?' Harriet asked.

'His lordship is still with Her Grace.'

Harriet felt totally unable to face Lord Richard yet, and behave as though nothing were different. Seeing him, knowing what he felt about her, would be a knife twisting in the wound her heart suffered.

'Pray tell Her Grace I have a slight headache. If Her Grace does not want me, I will rest here a while.'

So Harriet sat in her room undisturbed, struggling to control—at least outwardly—her feelings. From having been raised to a peak, she was now in the slough of despond, and it was some time before she was able to control her tears, and think with any degree of resolution.

But thought was hardly necessary for her to come to the decision that she must leave London. As much as she had wanted to leave Cumberland and Miss Bassenthwaite's school a few short weeks ago, so now she was equally anxious to return there—to the only home she had ever known.

No sooner did she realize this than Harriet set about thinking how she should accomplish her purpose. The fifteen shillings and four pence she had remaining was certainly far from sufficient to pay for her coach fare to Carlisle. How very foolish she had been when Mr Harcombe had offered to provide her with some pocket money! She should have accepted his offer to tide her over till her next allowance was due. Mid-summer Day was still some days away, and ideas buzzed through Harriet's head as to how she might raise the sum she needed.

When the usual light luncheon was due to be served, Harriet bathed her face and tidied her hair, and composed herself to go downstairs, feeling calmer now that she had decided how she should proceed. To her relief, Lord Richard had departed and Harriet was able to reply to the duchess's kind enquiries as to her health with adequate composure.

Lord Talaton came to Mersea Square later in the afternoon, and invited Harriet to drive with him in the Park.

'My cattle will really be able to show you their paces, Miss Devenish,' the viscount cried enthusiastically. 'They are rested again now, and quite raring to go.'

Harriet had seen Lord Talaton the previous day when he had come to apologize for his behavior after the *fête champêtre*, and was still suitably chastened by his irate uncle's strictures upon his conduct. But today he seemed to have recovered all his former ebullience.

'I know that my uncle is engaged at this time,' Lord Talaton went on, 'and my grandmamma will make no objection to a gentle ride in the Park, will you, ma'am?' And he turned to the duchess with an engaging grin.

'I am not at all sure that your uncle would allow it, after what happened on a previous occasion,' the duchess answered slowly.

'But I will not be taking any short cuts, ma'am,' Lord

126

Talaton wheedled. 'And Miss Devenish has never seen what my horses can really do.'

'Would you trust yourself with my grandson again, Harriet, my dear?'

By now, Harriet had had an idea, and would be glad to be able to speak to Lord Talaton alone. 'I *should* like to go very much, Your Grace—if you would permit it.'

'Then, I see no reason why not.'

Harriet went up to her room to make herself ready, and while there wrote a note addressed to the duchess, and propped it up on her dressing-table where it could be seen easily. Then she put on her bonnet, and draped her shawl about her shoulders. She stood for a moment in the doorway, looking at the room which had been hers since she had come to London, a rather sad smile curving her lips. Then resolutely Harriet closed the door and tripped downstairs, and kissed the duchess goodbye.

'I will see you when you return, my dear,' Her Grace said, and Harriet had to turn away to hide a conscious blush. 'And George—be careful!'

'Of course, ma'am!' Lord Talaton grinned.

In a very few moments, Harriet was seated beside the viscount, and they were bowling through Mersea Square on their way to Piccadilly. She sat agreeing to all Lord Talaton's encomiums about his chestnuts, while all the while she was revolving in her mind how she could broach the matter about which she must speak. Suddenly, it seemed a very difficult matter, whereas, when she had first thought of it, she had felt that all she had to do was put forward a simple request.

They joined the press of carriages waiting to get into the Park and Lord Talaton turned to Harriet with excited eyes.

'You will enjoy this, Miss Devenish. You are in for a great treat.'

Harriet smiled abstractedly. 'I am sure I am, my lord.'

'I would have asked you yesterday, ma'am, but my uncle was still frosty with me I thought it better not to. He really can burn a fellow up when he likes!'

'I am sorry you have had to suffer that fate, my lord.'

'Are you, Miss Devenish?' Lord Talaton smiled at her warmly. 'Would you say that we get on very well together, Miss Devenish?' he added after a moment.

'Certainly, my lord.'

'We like the same sort of things, do we not?'

'I—think so, my lord.'

'Fast horses, and waltzing—and things like that?'

'They are very exciting, my lord.'

'Yes, they are, are not they? Oh, Miss Devenish,' Lord Talaton went on very ardently, 'when I saw you being driven off in Rakewell's carriage, I can not tell you how I felt. It was like a drowning man going down. I saw before my eyes all the things we had done together.'

Harriet was struck now by what Lord Talaton was saying, and turned to give him her full attention. 'Did you indeed, my lord?' she asked, much struck.

'Indeed, I did, Miss Devenish! I was quite frantic with worry, as I said yesterday. Had anything happened to you, Miss Devenish, I-I think I should have gone mad! I told my uncle that too!'

'Luckily, my lord,' Harriet said soothingly, 'nothing did happen. Your-your uncle found me in time.' And suddenly Harriet had to blink to rid her eyes of tears.

'Yes, he did, didn't he?' Lord Talaton burst out now, frowning. 'And do you know, Miss Devenish, he would not take me with him! He positively refused and rode off, with never a word as to where he was going!''

'I expect he thought—you would wish to rest,' Harriet got out attempting to be diplomatic; 'after all, it can not have been pleasant, being knocked into the gorse bush . . . '

'But he should have taken me with him. After all, *I* had been with you! But he said—*he* was responsible, as your guardian, and that I—' Here the viscount broke off, and a red tide swept his cheeks.

Harriet murmured something incomprehensible, as her heart leapt a little with excitement.

They got into the Park at last, and then the press thinned and they were able to make a better speed. Lord Talaton urged his horses to a fast trot, and for a moment all conversation ceased as they rushed forward, the air blowing against their faces.

They made one complete circuit, then Lord Talaton slowed the horses and turned to Harriet. 'There, Miss Devenish! Was not that more like it!'

'It was very exciting, my lord!' For a few minutes, Harriet had actually forgotten her troubles in the exhilaration of speed.

'Oh, I knew you would like it, Miss Devenish! You really are a goer!' This was high praise indeed from Lord Talaton.

Harriet smiled back. 'Thank you, my lord.'

Without any warning, Lord Talaton suddenly seized Harriet's hand nearest to him. 'I had not meant to speak yet, Miss Devenish, but—dash it—I can not bear to wait any longer. When I think how my uncle spoke to me—! Miss Devenish! Let me be your guardian—in place of my uncle!' And the viscount looked at her with eyes that were more ardent than ever.

'I do not understand you, my lord!' Harriet returned, genuinely puzzled.

'I mean—marry me, Miss Devenish! Then you would no longer be subject to my uncle's direction. Oh, do say yes, Miss Devenish! We would have such fun—routs, and masquerades and endless schemes! I have never known a female I liked better than you, Miss Devenish! You always look delightfully, and you never dress down a fellow!'

Harriet tried to gather her wits together. She was certain that she had just heard Lord Talaton ask her to marry him, but her mind yet again seemed to have lost its customary efficiency. Indeed, she had not been listening too carefully, for not far ahead of them she had caught sight of Lord Richard's phaeton, and beside his lordship sat Lady Charlotte Logan, and she could hardly ask Lord Talaton to repeat himself!

With an effort she withdrew her gaze from the vehicle ahead and looked into Lord Talaton's face. The young man was still clutching her hand.

Now he seized her other hand. 'Dearest Miss Devenish! Do say yes!'

There could be no doubt about anything now. Harriet's heart started to thump against her ribs, and she attempted to withdraw her hands. 'Oh, my lord—!'

'You must know how I have felt, Miss Devenish—from the very first moment we met. You are the prettiest, most adorable creature in the whole of London, and—and if you do not say yes, I will shoot myself!' Lord Talaton ended wildly.

'I-I do not quite know what to say, my lord,' Harriet began, trying to find words with which to let down her ardent suitor kindly. She had not the least doubt what she should say. She had no wish to marry the viscount; he was great fun and she was very fond of him, and when she was with him she always enjoyed herself when he was not landing her in some terrible scrape—but—she could not see him as a husband. And in any case, she was not in love with him, but with—

'Say yes, dearest Miss Devenish!'

Harriet looked away from Lord Talaton's countenance for a moment, and her glance fell on the phaeton ahead. Lady Charlotte Logan had now linked her arm through Lord Richard's, and was laughing up into his face. At that moment, Lord Richard turned to his companion and smiled, and though Harriet was some distance away and could not see Lord Richard's expression clearly, from his whole way of leaning towards his fair companion it was plain to Harriet that he was looking into the face of the woman he loved. Harriet stared ahead and fought to keep back the hot tears which threatened to splash down her cheeks.

'Miss Devenish! Do speak to me! Tell me that you will marry me!'

As from a great distance Harriet heard Lord Talaton's voice, although in reality his mouth was only an inch or two from her ear.

Suddenly resolute, Harriet turned to him. 'Lord Talaton,' she began, her voice barely audible, 'I would be delighted to marry you!'

'You would! Oh, Miss Devenish! Dearest Miss Devenish! You have made me the happiest man in London!' And he carried Harriet's hands to his lips and covered them with kisses.

At that, there was quite a cheer from the bystanders, and Harriet looked round her with flaming cheeks. She saw that not only were they causing a traffic jam, for Lord Talaton had stopped in the middle of the track, and those held up behind were now shouting at them to move forward, but that they were the centre of attention also for those pedestrians nearby, many of whom had stopped and were now regarding them with laughing curiosity and good humour. Much agitated, Harriet tried again to draw her hands away. 'Oh, my lord! Pray let us continue!'

'Oh, Miss Devenish! Harriet!' Lord Talaton went on, taking not the slightest notice of Harriet or anybody else.

'My lord! Everyone is staring at us!'

'I do not care! I am glad for the whole world to know!'

'But I find it excessively uncomfortable, my lord!' Harriet cried urgently, her cheeks more crimson than ever.

'Oh, forgive me, Miss Devenish!' Lord Talaton released her hands then, and picked up the reins and flicked them so that the curricle sprang forward again.

Too late Harriet saw that they were going to overtake Lord Richard's phaeton. As they drew abreast, Lord Talaton reined in his horses a little so that the two carriages were proceeding side by side.

'Good day, Uncle!' the viscount cried exuberantly. 'Lady Charlotte.' Lord Talaton doffed his hat. 'Miss Devenish has just said that she will marry me! Pray give me your congratulations, Uncle!'

For the life of her, Harriet could not look at Lord Richard. She shivered as she heard his astonished exclamation. 'What! Is that true, Miss Devenish?'

With a quick little sideways glance Harriet nodded her head and muttered, 'Yes, my lord!'

Lady Charlotte's laughing voice now cried, 'Pray let *me* congratulate you, my lord; you have picked a charming bride! And Miss Devenish, my felicitations. I am sure you will both be very happy. Do not they make a charming young couple my lord?'

But Lord Richard offered no pleasant comment or word of congratulation. Instead he barked out, 'It is the most ridiculous thing I have ever heard! Miss Devenish, you nonsensical child! Have you indeed agreed to marry my addle-pated nephew?'

'Oh, here, I say, Uncle! That's coming it a bit strong!' Lord Talaton protested.

'Coming it a bit strong! That is the mildest thing I might say, you young whelp!' Lord Richard roared. He swept on, 'Have you forgot, Miss Devenish, what scrapes my nephew has led you into? Have you forgot—? 'Pon my soul, ma'am, I think you must be as addle-pated as my nephew himself!'

Harriet was stung to reply at that. 'Thank you, my lord,' she said tartly. 'As always you phrase yourself so delicately. I assure you that I am convinced that Lord Talaton and I will be very happy together.'

'Stuff and nonsense!' Lord Richard began on a roar.

But Lady Charlotte cried smoothly, 'Of course you will!' Then she turned to Lord Richard. 'Richard! You are scarcely kind to Miss Devenish and Lord Talaton! After all, am not I right in thinking that Miss Devenish has some claim upon your goodwill, being your ward? You should be glad that she has made such an excellent choice, marrying into your own family—your own sister's son! You should be pleased that she is to be set up so creditably.'

'I will not have it!' Lord Richard snapped, looking thunderous. 'I shall never give my consent.'

'Oh, but Uncle! You must! We can not wait so long!' Lord Talaton cried appalled.

'Never!' Lord Richard thundered again.

The two carriages had now been proceeding side by side for several minutes, and in that time they had succeeded in blocking the track leaving room for only one small vehicle to pass them. There were increasingly vociferous shouts and catcalls and demands that the track should be cleared.

Lord Talaton glanced behind him, and shouted with some relief, 'I think we had better go on now, Uncle. Good-day to you. Good-day, Lady Charlotte.' And he whipped up his chestnuts and the curricle dashed ahead.

'I'll see you later, you young—!' But the end of Lord Richard's sentence was lost to them.

Lord Talaton drove on in silence for some moments, then slowed the carriage a little and remarked, ''Pan my soul, Miss Devenish, I had not thought my uncle would cut up so very rough! After all, I am over twenty-one, and not even in debt!'

Harriet, whipping up her own anger against Lord Richard to suppress the desolation she felt at the core of her being agreed that Lord Richard had behaved in a very high-handed manner.

'I-I meant what I said, Miss Devenish,' Lord Talaton went on, made brave by Harriet's whole-hearted support. 'I should not care to wait so long till you are free of my uncle's charge.'

'No, indeed!' Harriet cried. 'But then there is no need—'

'Miss Devenish,' Lord Talaton interrupted agitatedly; 'Miss Devenish—Harriet—I see that my uncle will never agree. He is determined to keep his control over you for as long as ever he can. I see that plainly. But—what say you, Miss Devenish—Harriet—what say you to-to-eloping to Gretna Green—and so spiking my uncle's guns?'

And Lord Talaton stopped the carriage yet again and caught hold of Harriets's hands.

'Elope, my lord!' Harriet gasped, her eyes nearly starting out of her head.

'Yes, yes!' Lord Talaton warmed to his theme now that it was broached. 'Once we were married his power over you would be at an end. Oh, dearest Miss Devenish, can not you see that it is the only thing to be done? I really think it quite likely that my uncle would lock you up on bread and water, and forbid us to meet entirely, he is become such an old curmudgeon now. And, just think, dearest Miss Devenish, what a lark it would be! Can not you imagine my uncle's face when he found out that the knot was well and truly tied!'

'Indeed, I can, my lord! But, I do not think your uncle would lock me up,' Harriet went on, justice getting the better of her fading anger with Lord Richard. But then her mind's eye returned to the vision of Lord Richard smiling down into Lady Charlotte's upturned face, and a wave of desolation swept over her. Yes! Once she was married to Lord Talaton, she would have her own establishment, and she would not need to see Lord Richard very often, and in any case, he would be married also, and she did like Lord Talaton very much, and it was quite true when he said that they got on excellently well. And—she would not have a dull life—that was certain.

Lord Talaton meanwhile had been urging his idea more vigorously than ever. Now Harriet turned to him, her mind made up. 'I think it an excellent idea, my lord. It would solve all our problems. Let us set out for Gretna at once!'

'Oh, Miss Devenish! Oh, Harriet! I always said you were a goer!'

Eight

Almost before she had gathered her wits about her, Harriet found herself in a hired chaise, rattling along the road to the north. Once she had made up her mind to go with Lord Talaton, Harriet was anxious to be off at once; she had declared that she wished to take nothing with her: anything needful might be purchased upon the journey; and to her relief Lord Talaton had behaved with singular expedition, and she had been in a whirl while he made all the arrangements. This suited Harriet very well, for it meant that she had not the least second in which to think.

'We will send a note when we are well upon our way,' Lord Talaton said excitedly. 'We do no want any one to worry, but, if we send it too soon, they may catch up with us.' Harriet said nothing of the note she had already left for the duchess—not because she did not wish to upset Lord Talaton, but because it quite slipped her memory.

Lord Talaton's tiger had been despatched home with the curricle and the chestnuts, and a coachman had been secured for the first stage, and by half-past six the two were embarked upon their journey.

The viscount was in a high state of excitement, and Harriet herself endeavoured to keep her spirits up, telling herself that this plan was but little different from her original one; then she had meant to ask Lord Talaton to lend her the money for the stage. Now she was in a hired chaise—and with the protection of a friend, instead of being at the mercy of strangers.

But still, Harriet could not help but feel grave doubts, being very far from certain that she was doing right. Quite apart from the fact that eloping in itself was a distinctly havey—cavey action which, when it was known, could not but bring down the disapprobation of all respectable people upon her head, but—she became less and less sure that she could actually go through with the marriage to Lord Talaton. She shut her eyes to cut out the vision of the duchess's disappointed face when she learnt what Harriet had done, and felt alarming tears when she remembered Lord Richard. What a way to repay them!

Lord Talaton however remained exuberant. 'Oh, is not this capital, Miss Devenish, Harriet?' he cried excitedly. 'What a surprise my uncle will have when he finds out! We will wait till we get up into Bedfordshire, I think, before we send any message.'

They changed horses at Horne's in Barnet, and for once Lord Talaton was loud in praise for horses other than his own. 'These are not bad cattle at all, are they, Miss Devenish? If they are all as good as these, we shall be at the Border in very short order!'

They had indeed been lucky at Barnet. The horses put to there were as fine as could be expected for hire. But then, Horne was the proprietor of one of the greatest coaching stables in England. They changed next at St. Albans, where a new coachman joined them, and the viscount continued highly pleased.

'I declare we might arrive in only five days at this rate, dearest Miss Devenish!' He paused for a moment, then said happily, 'I suppose this is a sort of home-coming for you, is not it?'

Harriet nodded and forced a smile, thinking of the last time she had been upon that road. Then she had been all excitement at the prospect of getting to London. On this return journey, she felt quite otherwise.

Dark had begun to fall, and with it Harriet's spirits descended even lower. She stared out of the window at the darkening countryside, horribly conscious now that she was quite alone with Lord Talaton, and that she would have to pass the night with him. It was very odd, but she had not the least recollection of feeling any such embarrassment when she had come to London with Lord Richard—and she had hardly known him!

Abruptly Harriet knew that she could not go through with it. 'Pray stop the horses my lord!' she cried.

'Stop, dearest Miss Devenish! What do you mean?'

'I-I can not go, my lord! I am sorry, but—I must go back to London. I can not go to Gretna with you!'

'But Miss Devenish! Harriet! What can you mean?' Lord Talaton's voice was high with astonishment.

'I am sorry,' Harriet repeated wretchedly, but more urgently, 'I-I just can not go on. Oh, pray, my lord, stop the horses and let us turn back without delay!'

'It is not surprising that you should feel so, my dearest love,' Lord Talaton began, kindly encouraging, and trying to take her hands.

But Harriet drew back, and cried out, 'I have made a mistake, my lord! I am indeed sorry, but I just can not do it! Please, please let us return to London at once!'

Now Lord Talaton said in a voice which was a nice

mixture of astonishment and offended pride, 'You mean—you do not wish to marry me, Miss Devenish?'

Harriet nodded miserably. 'I can never tell you how sorry I am, but—it would not do, my lord! Indeed, it would not do at all!'

'But you led me to believe—!'

'I know! And I was very wrong! But, oh, pray let us turn back before it is too late!'

'I must say, Miss Devenish,' Lord Talaton said very stiffly now, 'this is deuced queer behaviour!'

'Oh, I know it, my lord! I am all too well aware of it!'

'But—you told me that you wished to return to Cumberland in any case!'

'I know it, sir! I know it! But—not like this!'

Lord Talaton did knock on the roof then, and soon the coach halted, and Lord Talaton gave directions for them to turn back to the metropolis. The coachman quite audibly muttered something about some people being unable to make up their minds, but the coach did turn, and it was with relief that Harriet settled back against the squabs as they retraced their way.

Lord Talaton sat as far from her as he could in the far corner, arms folded, glaring out of the window into the darkness outside. Harriet was wretchedly conscious of his mood, and feeling that she had behaved very badly by him, she sought for some means to bring him round.

'It really would not have done, my lord, you must see that,' she said at last, very tremulously. '*I* was indeed addle-pated to agree to such a plan,' she added in an undertone, self-beratingly.

Lord Talaton only grunted for reply.

'It-it is not that I am not very-very fond of you, my lord,' Harriet continued timidly.

Lord Talaton turned to her eagerly and sought for her hand. 'Well, then, Miss Devenish! We may do it properly—wait till you are free of my uncle—none of this havey-cavey stuff—!'

'But—I do not think that we should agree very well together, my lord.'

'Why ever not!'

'Because—I do not think that you love me as—as a husband should—!' Harriet began.

'Oh, dearest Miss Devenish! What are you saying? I do! I do!' And Lord Talaton did succeed in clutching Harriet's hands.

But she shook her head. 'No. We have fun together, my lord, but—I know that I do not love you as a wife should love her husband. Besides, this—ramshackle way of doing things is not a good way to start a marriage, now, is it, my lord?'

'But I tell you, we will do it all according to Jorrocks. Hanover Square and the bishop in his mitre and—'

What other accoutrements Lord Talaton might have held out as an inducement to a regular marriage Harriet was not to hear for at that moment there was the loud, sharp sound of a crack and abruptly the carriage tipped over to one side accompanied by the noise of splitting wood and the squeals of terrified horses.

In the moment it took for Harriet to be flung to the floor, she had the feeling that she had lived through this moment before.

'What is that, my lord?' she shrieked, as she hit the floor of the carriage, and Lord Talaton came crashing on top of her.

'Miss Devenish! Are you all right?' Lord Talaton endeavoured to heave himself up, but slithered onto her again.

But the carriage had come to a rest, and the noise of the frightened horses was less as the coachman spoke soothingly to them. With an effort Lord Talaton managed to let down the coach window on the side nearer the ground, and sticking his head out, he shouted for help.

'In a moment, sir,' the coachman returned, still busy with the horses.

'Deuce take it, sir! We are all in a heap in here! The lady might have been killed. What has happened?'

'The near hind wheel must've cracked, sir. There, now, whoah. Whoah.'

Somehow, with Harriet lending what aid she could, Lord Talaton scrambled through the window, then turned to help out Harriet herself.

'Are you sure you are all right, Miss Devenish? You are not hurt?'

'Only bruised, my lord, I think,' Harriet returned unsteadily. 'But do go and help with the horses.'

'Are you quite certain nothing is broken?'

'Quite sure, my lord.'

Still shaking, Harriet sat down on the grass, and Lord Talaton went to do what he could to assist the coachman. One of the carriage lamps had been broken and the candle had blown out, but the other was undamaged, and now Lord Talaton brought it round so that they could see where to untangle the traces to release the horses.

Luckily the animals had suffered nothing more than some cuts and bruising. One of the leaders had nearly fallen, but had just managed to keep his feet, and the others had remained standing. Now the coachman proposed to go forward with two of the horses to the next town and return with another vehicle. The remaining two horses would be left with Harriet and Lord Talaton so that they might ride forward to meet the returning coachman if they wished.

As the man rode off, Harriet's mind darted back to the very recent occasion when she had found herself in exactly the same predicament. But on this occasion they were farther from home, and it was already dark, though, being on the main road, they might encounter other travellers.

'Well, Miss Devenish, what would you wish to do?' Lord Talaton demanded. 'Wait here, or shall we go forward?'

'I am hardly dressed for riding, my lord,' Harriet murmured, endeavouring to stifle an inopportune desire to laugh.

'My dear Miss Devenish! This is not a time to be concerned—!'

The idea that his lordship should be accusing her of frivolity now was the final straw. Harriet let out a great shriek of laughter, and Lord Talaton bent down towards her anxiously.

'Miss Devenish! Miss Devenish!'

Tears streamed now down Harriet's face. 'Oh, my lord!' she gasped, 'I do not know that I could sit a horse without a saddle!'

'Well, I will lift you up, Miss Devenish, and you may hang on to the mane . . . ' Lord Talaton looked somewhat doubtful.

'I will try, my lord,' Harriet murmured, brushing away her laughter tears.

Lord Talaton holding the horses' heads was a step or two away from Harriet. Now Harriet got to her feet, and brushed her skirt down. However, the light from the remaining carriage lamp was not directed towards her, and in the dark she stumbled over a tussock and gave her ankle a sad wrench. With a little cry, Harriet sank down again at the side of the road, all desire to laugh abruptly quenched.

'What is it, Miss Devenish? What has happened?'

'My ankle, my lord! I have twisted it!'

'Oh, let me help you!' Lord Talaton cried, looking about for somewhere to tie the horses.

'No, no! I shall be all right in a moment, my lord,' Harriet urged, rubbing her afflicted joint. 'I will just rest a moment or two.' Already her ankle felt hot and puffy to her fingers.

Lord Talaton continued solicitous, but at a short distance, still holding the horses, and Harriet remained reassuring, though the injured joint was seared with pain if she so much as wriggled her toes.

They stayed so for nearly twenty minutes after the coachman had left them. Once or twice Harriet had tried to rise, but she could not bear any weight on the twisted ankle. Night had fallen entirely now; there was not even a pale glow along the horizon, and had it not been for the light from the lamp, everywhere would have been black indeed. No other travellers passed them, and everywhere seemed heavy with stillness.

Harriet strained her ears, hoping for the sound of the returning coachman, but apart from Lord Talaton, all she heard were the usual night squeaks and calls of nocturnal birds and beasts. An owl hooting just above her head startled her, and some unearthly cry farther away made her think of souls in torment.

'I-I do hope the coachman will not be long now, my lord,' she quavered after one particularly blood-curling scream.

'It is some distance to the town, I dare say, but he should

be returned soon.' The viscount paused. 'If he does return at all,' he added darkly.

'My lord! W-what do you mean?'

'That unfortunately we have no guarantee that we shall not be left to make shift for ourselves. I promised the fellow some guineas, but they may not weigh enough against the attractions of his comfortable bed.'

'Oh, my lord, do not suggest such a thing! You mean, we might be left here all night!'

'Unless you can ride one of these, Miss Devenish.'

The idea of remaining outside under the sky all night, a prey to any malefactor who might pass that way, did more to rouse Harriet's determination than anything else.

'Well, it seems I *must* do it, my lord!' And gingerly Harriet made to stand up. The pain was excruciating, and she stifled a yelp as she put her weight on the damaged ankle.

But she was only half-way up when there came through the night air the sound of galloping hooves. Harriet froze, thinking now of a highwayman, rather than of a genuine traveller like themselves. 'Did you hear that, my lord?' she whispered fearfully.

'A horseman coming towards us, Miss Devenish,' Lord Talaton pronounced in a normal voice.

'Suppose it is—!' Harriet gasped.

'What, Miss Devenish?'

'A-a highwayman,' Harriet squeaked in reply.

'A highwayman would not approach us so, but would spring out on us as silently as he could,' Lord Talaton pointed out patiently.

But Harriet was not convinced. In fact she was positively persuaded that it was someone who would cut their throats without a moment's hesitation and leave them both dead in a ditch.

The horseman was much nearer now, and Harriet's heart thudded in her breast. 'What shall we do, my lord? Where can we hide?'

'There is no need to hide, Miss Devenish,' Lord Talaton said stoutly. 'And if by any chance it be a highwayman, I am quite able to deal with him. Pray do not fear, ma'am; I will see that you come to no harm.'

Harriet could make no answer to that, but unbidden into her mind slipped the memory of those previous occasions when she had been with Lord Talaton, and he had proved powerless to help her. Oh, if only Lord Richard were her companion now! Then she would not have the least fear.

Only a short distance now lay between themselves and the fast-approaching horseman. In another second feeble gleams from the lantern showed the legs of a horse which was slowed at once on coming up to them.

A voice cried out, 'Who is there?'

'Stranded travellers' Lord Talaton shouted back. 'The wheel of our carriage is broken and—'

But he got no further, for his jaw dropped in astonishment. The horseman had reined in and was jumping to the ground. As he turned to his horse's head, Harriet, who had somehow hobbled into the road, gave a cry and flung herself into his arms. 'Oh, my lord! My lord!' she sobbed. 'I am so thankful it is you!'

'Harriet! Oh, my dear!' Lord Richard cried, and the next moment she felt his arms about her and she was safe in his embrace.

Lord Talaton, momentarily shocked, now stuttered, 'U— Uncle! Is it-r-r-really you?'

'Of course it is, you addle—pated young greenhead,

you!' Lord Richard returned in a vexed voice, not in the least slackening his hold of Harriet.

'But—how came you to find us!' Lord Talaton gasped, still amazed at the sudden appearance of his irate kinsman.

'Miss Devenish had the wit to leave a note for the duchess saying that she was going to Cumberland. What should I do but come after her? But, you did not say that you were going in company with this reprobate nephew of mine,' Lord Richard added, suddenly holding Harriet away from him, and though she could hardly see, Harriet felt that he was gazing at her very sternly. 'Really, Miss Devenish, it seems that I can not let you out of my sight for one moment but that you must get yourself involved in my nephew's harum—scarum schemes!'

'I-I did not mean to be with your nephew then, my lord!' Harriet gasped. 'There-there was some rearrangement later.'

'So I collect!' Lord Richard's voice was hard and he gripped Harriet tightly by the shoulders. 'And, may I ask, why was it that you chose my nephew as a travelling companion and not myself?'

'Miss Devenish could hardly think to marry you, Uncle!' Lord Talaton broke in, feeling he should make some contribution to the discussion.

'Marry! What has marry to do with it?' Lord Richard roared.

'We were going to Gretna, Uncle,' Lord Talaton returned with dignity.

Harriet felt Lord Richard's fingers tighten still more on her shoulders. 'Is this true, Miss Devenish?' he demanded harshly.

'Yes, my lord,' Harriet mumbled shamefaced. 'But—we

146

had turned round, my lord, a little before the wheel broke,' she added pleadingly.

Lord Richard's fingers relaxed a fraction. 'And why was that?'

Harriet could not answer, but Lord Talaton said somewhat huffily, 'Miss Devenish felt it better to return.'

'Well! I am glad one of you had some sense! Miss Devenish, whatever were you thinking of? And—why should you wish to return to Cumberland in any case?'

That was something else Harriet could not answer, and she hung her head, though her blushing cheeks could not be seen in the darkness. Lord Talaton was unable to answer that one either.

'Well, we had better get on,' Lord Richard said after a moment. 'Or were you prepared to camp here all night?'

'Our coachman is gone to fetch another vehicle,' Lord Talaton returned with dignity.

'Well, why in heaven's name did you set forward to meet it?'

'I-I have twisted my ankle, my lord!' Harriet explained. 'I can scarcely walk.'

'Can not you?' Lord Richard demanded, looking down at Harriet. '*I* would never have thought—' He stopped, then said, 'You had better ride with me, then. Talaton, you may bring on that pair.'

And without waiting for Harriet to say a word, Lord Richard swung her onto his horse and in a trice was up behind her himself. His arms came round her as he held the reins, and thoroughly tired now, and quite shameless, Harriet nestled against Lord Richard's chest, only too thankful to let him take charge of everything.

Lord Talaton muttered something, but did as his uncle bid him, and they made a silent little cavalcade back to the

147

town. Lord Richard occasionally asked Harriet if she was all right, and Harriet each time murmured that she was quite all right, thinking to herself that she wished the ride might go on forever. Bother Lady Charlotte! For the moment it was she, Harriet, who was encircled by Lord Richard's arms, and it was bliss indeed. Lord Talaton brought up the rear with the two carriage horses.

They came upon no coachman returning with a carriage, and for some odd reason, Lord Richard forebore to mention it.

When they reached the town, Lord Richard hired a chaise and coachman, and bade Lord Talaton bring his own horse back to London, when he had settled what should be done about the broken chaise. 'But slowly, mind, Talaton,' he admonished 'In fact, it would be better if you remained here for the night and came on in the morning.'

'I would rather get back to London tonight, Uncle! I have no liking for this provincial hostelry.'

'I dare say you would! But have some thought for my horse! You will wait here till tomorrow, and if I find you returned before noon, I'll—well, I'll call you out!'

Though Lord Talaton knew perfectly well that the threat was an idle one, he still retained enough respect for his uncle's tongue to agree without further argument.

So Harriet and Lord Richard rolled out of the innyard, and Lord Talaton remained behind to cool his heels and believe that he had been very badly used.

Harriet felt horridly shy as she was shut into the carriage, and sat as far away from Lord Richard as she possibly could. She remembered the brazen way in which she had clung to him while riding before him, and now she blushed to think what Lord Richard must have thought of her. There was a silence between he two of them for some time, and for once Harriet felt far too shy to break it.

148

But at last Lord Richard himself spoke. 'Well, Miss Devenish?' he said in a weary voice.

'Well, my lord?' Harriet whispered.

'So—you are in love with my nephew?'

'Oh, no, my lord!' Harriet's voice came hotly in reply. 'Not!'

'No!'

'Then—why elope to Gretna, you—nonsensical child?'

'Because Lord Talaton asked me to!'

'Are you trying to say that you would elope with any man who asked you?'

'No, of course not!'

'Then—?'

'Lord Talaton said that you would never agree to our marrying, and as he could not wait till I was free of you, we should elope—'

'He was quite right! I should never have agreed!'

'There you are then!'

'But—have you forgot—I have no right to agree or disagree, Miss Devenish?' Lord Richard said again in that weary voice. 'Why did not you tell my nephew that it did not matter what I said?'

'I started to once—but the subject changed, and—I did not think to do so again.'

There was another silence between them. This time it was Harriet who broke it. 'But—I could not go through with it, my lord. Even to get to Cumberland, which was all I meant to do at first. We turned round to come back to London, my lord.'

'I remember you said it before.'

'But it is true!'

'I know it is.'

'How?'

'Your carriage was turned towards London.'

'Oh, I see.'

Somehow Harriet felt deflated then. She sat back and tried to think of something else to say.

'Why did you want to go to Cumberland, Miss Devenish? You had only to ask and I would have been happy to take you there,' Lord Richard said sadly at last. When Harriet made no answer, he went on, more melancholy than ever, 'Did you really want to be free of me, Miss Devenish?'

'Oh, no, my lord!' Harriet's cry came from her heart. 'I-I thought that it was you who wanted to be free of me!'

'What *do* you mean, Miss Devenish?'

'You said to Her Grace that I-I was encumbrance!' Harriet's voice could scarcely be heard.

'Never!'

'I heard you, my lord!'

'When was this?'

'When we came back from seeing Mr Harcombe the other—I mean, this morning!' Harriet returned, thinking that it seemed a year ago since she had sat in Mr Harcombe's office and learnt that she was to receive an allowance still.

'But I did not mean—I meant that perhaps it was too much to expect Her Grace—*I* had no wish to see you gone!' And Lord Richard turned to Harriet, and took her hands, and looked at her very seriously.

'Oh!' Harriet felt like weeping, so happy did she suddenly feel. His lordship did not want to be rid of her after all! 'Is that why—I mean—why would you never have agreed to my marrying your nephew?' she asked breathlessly.

'Because, my dear Miss Devenish, I could not bear to

see you married to anyone but myself!' Lord Richard said firmly.

'Oh! What did you say, my lord?' Harriet gasped in a very small voice, hardly able to believe her ears.

'I said that I could not bear to see you married to anyone but myself!' Lord Richard repeated more firmly.

'But—what of Lady Charlotte?' Harriet cried, almost dizzy with happiness.

'Lady Charlotte! What of Lady Charlotte?'

'Are not—you in love with her?'

'Good heavens no!'

'I-I am certain that she wishes to marry you!'

'That may be true, Miss Devenish,' Lord Richard answered ungallantly; 'but I do not in the least wish to marry her!'

'Oh, my lord! I thought you did!'

'But—why?—Whatever—?' Suddenly Lord Richard was very close to Harriet and had possessed himself firmly of both her hands. 'Is that why you wanted to go back to Cumberland, you—nonsensical child? Because you thought—?'

Harriet nodded happily.

'And *I* thought you were in love with my addle—pated nephew!'

Harriet shook her head tenderly. 'Never, my lord! Not for a moment. I always thought of you, my lord, when I needed to be rescued!'

'And you would permit me, Miss Devenish, to keep you safe always?' Lord Richard asked now, very tenderly.

'I have always said that I felt safe with you, my lord. Do not you remember—that first time we met? After all, you must recall that it was I who chose you for my guardian!'

The next moment, Harriet was in Lord Richard's embrace, and he was murmuring against her hair, 'Oh, you—nonsensical child!' as he held her to him.

The rest of the journey passed all too swiftly. They had a thousand things to say to each other—a thousand questions to ask and answer, and not half of them had been spoken by the time the chaise rolled into Mersea Square.

As the vehicle stopped, Harriet cried, much embarrassed now, 'Oh, what will Her Grace think of me! She must think me so ungrateful!'

'My mamma will be only too happy to have you safe home again, my dearest love!'

'But—will she mind that—that we shall be—I mean—'

'That will make her happier than ever! She will be thankful that I am to settle down!'

'But—she does not know who I am! I mean—I might be anybody, and—well, one day you might be a duke!'

'And you will be the most beautiful duchess—if that day ever comes!'

'Do you think so? Do you really? But it would be better if we knew certain that my Papa was at least—a gentleman!'

'And my Mamma is convinced that he is!'

'You mean—was, my lord!'

'I mean-I mean—only a gentleman would use Drummond's Bank, my love! My Mamma is convinced that your father is—but she may tell you herself.'

And Lord Richard jumped from the carriage and helped Harriet down.

'My lord, you must tell me! I am in a fever of impatience! Has Her Grace had further news?'

Lord Richard laughed. 'You must wait to hear from her

own lips. But all I will say is, she has picked upon a gentleman who is—among the highest in the land!'

Harriet stared, and Lord Richard drew her up the steps to the front door, laughing. 'Who, my lord?'

Lord Richard's eyes were dancing. 'Do not you recall what Mr Harcombe said about a very *princely* sum?'

Before Harriet could answer, the door was flung open by Carruthers, and Her Grace came forward to take Harriet in her arms. 'Oh, my dear Harriet! Thank God you are home again!'

'I can promise you one thing, Mamma! This nonsensical child will never leave us again!' Lord Richard smiled, as he put his arms about both the women.

True romance
is <u>not</u> hard to find...
you need only look
as far as
FAWCETT BOOKS